My Big Gay Family Christmas Fiasco

Alex Leslie

Published by Alex Leslie, 2022.

MY BIG GAY FAMILY CHRISTMAS FIASCO

First edition. March 1, 2022.

ISBN: 979-8201378738

Written by Alex Leslie.

Chapter One – Charlie Hates Christmas

I HATE CHRISTMAS.

Okay, so I don't object to Christmas in theory. As a child, the young Charlie Nolan didn't have a problem with Christmas at all. That's because, like most children, my involvement in the season did not extend beyond opening presents and playing with toys.

As an adult, the basic sentiments behind the holiday are all well and good. The season for giving; goodwill to all men; Mariah Carey belting out a modern yet traditional festive song that is as uplifting as it is infectious.

All of these are good as far as I'm concerned. The real issue is that in thirty years of yuletide joy that I have experienced so far, I am yet to have had one Christmas season that did not devolve into a screeching, over-emotional psychodrama. And why?

My family.

Don't get me wrong. I love my family dearly. I've just never really fit in with them. I've always felt like the odd man out. Not because I'm gay, mind you, as my little sister is also of the homosexual persuasion. But I've never really been one for massive emotional outbursts, whether they be public or private. Nor have I felt the need to turn any given situation into a scene out of a Mexican soap opera. Also, I've never been much of a drinker, so getting absolutely shitfaced with the rest of the tribe has never been high on my holiday 'must-do' list. Plus, despite decades of my father desperately trying to spark my interest in the game, I couldn't care less about test match cricket, much to his chagrin.

But my number one problem with the Christmas season? Every year, I get to spend four days at my parent's house with our extended family. Four days of Mum's obsessive attempts to create the 'perfect' family Christmas celebration by regimenting every single moment with activities and events, all while the rest of the family do everything in their power to resist against her tyrannical devotion to her holiday lists and schedules. Mum should have learned by now that no amount of scheduling was going to be enough to reign in the craziness that is our family, and that any attempt to do so was ultimately doomed to failure.

A Nolan Family Christmas is a bit like a swirling portal to Hell. You know, going in, that it's going to be awful. But nothing can prepare you for the screaming, crying or lethal fruit mince pies. But over the years, just like death and taxes, I have come to accept it as one of life's unavoidable fixtures.

As I sat at my desk at work, a spreadsheet on the screen in front of me becoming nothing more than a jumbled mass of numbers and symbols, I was broken from my reverie by a familiar voice.

"Charlie, Earth to Charlie!"

I looked up from my laptop to see the voluptuous form of my colleague and best friend, Bree Anderson, standing in my open doorway.

"Sorry, hun. I was miles away. Did you need something?"

"Yeah, it's coffee time. Let's go!" Bree said, and without another word, turned away and walked toward the staff break room. I logged out of my computer and followed her.

When I reached the break room, Bree was already making two cups of steaming magic wake-up juice, so I headed to the snack cupboard to find some goodies. One great thing about working for a government department, the break rooms are always well-stocked. I found an unopened packet of Tim Tams buried under a pile of assorted rice crackers.

Score!

As I took my first sip of coffee and bit into one of the delectable chocolate biscuits, I found my earlier mood slowly ebbing away.

"So, what's up with you?" Bree said without preamble, "You've been out of sorts for days."

"Oh, it's nothing serious. It's just the end of the year…"

"Holiday blues?" She said, nodding sympathetically.

"Sort of. Mum rang the other day, and there's no chance of me getting out of Christmas this year. My older brother, Craig, is still on deployment god knows where overseas. If we're lucky, we might get a brief video message from him sometime before New Year. Plus my little sister, Charmaine, is at University in Queensland, so she's spending the holidays with her girlfriend's family. That leaves me as the only one of the kids who'll be at Christmas this year."

"Bugger."

"That's not all. Mum's up to something. She was asking me all sorts of questions. Wanting to know if I was seeing anyone or planning on bringing a date for Christmas. I smell another one of her horrible holiday blind date fix ups on the horizon."

"Good! You need to get your dick wet."

"Bree!" I said, scandalised.

"What? You do! When was the last time you had a date?"

"It's not easy, you know. I work insane hours. When do I have time for a social life?"

"If it's important, you make the time. Besides, I think you use work as an excuse to get out of social stuff. Nobody does the kind of extra hours you do. Cut back and live a little. Maybe your Mum's blind date will be cute?"

I burst out laughing. Bree had *no idea* how bad my mother was at matchmaking.

"The last time my Mum fixed me up with a guy, it was her hairdresser. After an excruciatingly awkward date, he eventually confessed he was straight! The only reason he agreed to go out with me was that Mum was a big tipper and he was afraid of offending her by saying no. He made me swear on a stack of bibles that I wouldn't tell her the truth! It was a total disaster."

Bree took a moment to process this, then burst out laughing.

"Besides, I've never really had much luck with dating. I've only ever had one serious boyfriend, and you know how that turned out." I returned to my coffee and grabbed another Tim Tam. There's nothing like the Christmas season to make me eat my feelings.

This time of year never seemed to fail to remind me of my failure to bounce back after the whole Liam thing.

Liam.

It was over eight years ago. He was my first serious boyfriend. My first lover. My first heartbreak. The two of us clicked from the very start. Our differences complimented each other and we enjoyed each other's company so easily. We were together for just over six months, and well on the track to moving in together. I pictured us getting married, growing old together – the whole package.

Then suddenly, the whole relationship fell apart in the space of a few weeks. Liam started cancelling dinner dates. He would be 'stuck in traffic' or would 'suddenly have to work late at the last minute' which, initially, I understood. We both worked busy, demanding jobs. But then the 'last-minute business trips' started. We went from spending so much time together to little more than trading voicemails.

Then one day I got the phone call from his boss, asking if I could get a message to Liam. Given that Liam was away on a business trip, and he'd told me he was going with his boss, I really didn't know what to say. Now that I had caught him out in a lie, it started to make me wonder what else he was lying about. Suddenly all the cancelled dates and late nights at the office made sense.

He was cheating on me.

Like I said earlier, I'm not one for big emotional outbursts or dramatic confrontations. So when Liam finally deigned to get in contact with me, I simply told him that I felt things weren't working out between us and that I felt we should see other people. The fact that he already had a head start was neither here nor there. To give him credit, Liam did put on a good show of being shocked, but he never made any attempt to defend himself or, more importantly, apologise for his transgressions. He certainly didn't make any effort to fight to keep our relationship going, which was all the confirmation I needed.

So we called it a day and move on with our lives. No mess. No fuss. I never saw or heard from him again.

For weeks after, I just walked around in a heartbroken daze. It wasn't until I met Bree on her first day of work and we became fast friends, that I was able to shake off the mood and get back to some sense of normality.

But from that point forward, any time I go on a date with a man, I couldn't help but subconsciously compare them to Liam. Not the cheating slime ball who broke my heart, but the Liam I clicked with on our first date; the Liam that was so easy to talk to. The Liam who was the other half of me. I've never found that instant connection and comfort with anyone else.

"Charlie!" Bree snapped me out of my reverie again.

"Sorry. I spaced out again."

"If you don't want to get fixed up by your Mum, why don't you just tell her no?"

"Saying 'no' to Kathleen Nolan isn't as easy as you'd think. She's like a steamroller. It'd be easier to tell the trees not to grow or the wind not to blow..."

"Oh. My. God! Are you quoting The Village People?" Bree said, sounding almost incredulous.

Jeez, was I quoting The Village People? I did listen to *You Can't Stop The Music* in the car this morning...

"No, of course not. Don't be ridiculous!" I said, praying Bree wouldn't pick up her phone and Google the lyrics. She eyed me suspiciously.

"Anyway, I wanted to ask you something," Bree said, looking a little shy all of a sudden, "Would it be weird if I asked to join you for Christmas with your family this year?"

I looked at Bree like she had grown a second head. I've told her stories of Nolan Family Christmases. Did she think I was lying?

"Have you lost your mind? Why would you want to subject yourself to that?"

"My parents are going to Bali for the holidays and I don't have anywhere to go for Christmas..."

"Why not tag along with them. The office is closed until after New Year. It'd be a great little getaway for you."

"Well, I already suggested that to my parents and Mum made it clear that my presence would not be welcome. In her words: 'Mummy and Daddy need their special hugging time' End quote."

"Ew."

"I know, right?"

"I'll lay a lot of things at my parent's door, but they've never said anything as revolting as 'special hugging time.' Oh, god. I think I'm going to be sick." I fanned myself, trying to get some fresh air.

"So please, don't leave me alone. Let me come along. I've always wanted to experience a Christmas with your family for myself. All those stories. It sounds like it's going to be a blast."

Silly Rabbit.

She really does think I was exaggerating. She thinks this is just going to be a slightly less formal Christmas than she's used to with her family. She's just signed her own death warrant.

"Alright, you can come. But on one condition."

"Name it!" Bree said, bouncing with enthusiasm.

"Christmas with the Nolan family is not a spectator sport. There's no sitting on the sidelines and no 'get out of jail free' cards. If you're in, you're all in." I said, adding as much gravitas to my voice as humanly possible.

"Deal!"

"And may God have mercy on your soul..." I said under my breath as she dashed around the table to give me an awkward hug from behind.

Chapter Two – There's No Place Like Hell

Christmas Eve Eve *(definition)*

An entirely unofficial and non-existent holiday celebrated by my parents. Held on December 23rd each year, Christmas Eve Eve is treated as an 'introduction' to the Nolan Family Christmas festivities because, apparently, the three officially recognised Christmas holidays don't generate enough chaos for our family.

I ARRIVED AT Bree's place at around nine A.M. on Christmas Eve Eve, her small duplex only a few streets away from my house. My old but reliable Toyota Camry was loaded up with my luggage and Christmas gifts, with more than enough room for Bree to stow her stuff in the boot too. When I pulled into her driveway, I gave the horn a quick beep and, moments later, Bree emerged juggling suitcases.

It still surprised me how different she was outside of work. Gone were the sensible corporate outfits, tight and tidy hair piled in a neat bun, and perfect makeup. Off the clock, Bree looked like she owned a tattoo shop. I watched her in the rear vision mirror as she loaded her stuff in the boot. Dressed in her standard ripped black jeans, a white crop top that showed off the ink on her arms and chest, and her shimmering raven hair flowing wild and free, Bree had softened her casual look slightly for the occasion by wearing a small brooch on her top. When she got into the car, I got a closer look at the accessory and discovered it was Santa riding his sleigh.

Bree outside of work wasn't just a cosmetic change. At work, Bree tended to be very prim and proper. She would get her job done with a minimum of gossip, avoided office politics, and was a stickler for professionalism and following the rules.

Outside of work, Bree was a wild woman.

My friend was all about thrill-seeking. Riding motorcycles, going skydiving, white water rafting. Anything to get an adrenaline high. In almost every way, Bree was my total opposite. While she was having the adventure, I was happy sitting on the sidelines watching her have fun. She was welcome to the drama and excitement. I was content to stay out of the way.

Once buckled in, we were on our way. The trip from Melbourne to the Mornington Peninsula would usually take about an hour or so, given good traffic conditions. To my eternal chagrin, a total lack of natural disasters or Godzilla attacks meant that traffic was light and we arrived at my parent's house more or less on time. My mother would accept nothing less than a Category 6 cyclone or a giant radioactive reptile onslaught as a reasonable excuse for skipping out on Christmas.

The Nolan family home, a two-storey, six-bedroom ocean-front home, was in one of the nicer suburbs in the area. While not rich per-se, my parents had always been more than comfortable thanks to my Dad's career as a FIFO worker in various mines in Western Australia. Kevin Nolan would fly out, stay at the mine for days or even weeks at a time, then return home for a break. During the mining boom, the pay was exceptional, and he was able to easily afford their exceptionally beautiful home by the water. Thanks to some good investments, Dad was able to retire early and enjoy the fruits of his spoils before he 'got too old' - in his words.

As we pulled up in front of the house, the first thing I noticed was my father up on a tall ladder, threading what appeared to be a truly disturbing amount of twinkle lights onto the front of the eaves. He was shirtless, showing off what had once been a trim and taught figure, now softened considerably since he retired. His years underground in the mines had not prepared his pale, milky skin for the harshness of the Summer sun and, despite Mum's endless nagging for him to 'slip slop slap,' his back was looking disturbingly pink. Although, realistically, I should probably have been more concerned about the pile of empty beer bottles laying at the base of the ladder.

"Hi, Dad!" I called out as I stepped out of the car. My father did not turn around, focussed entirely on undoing a knot in the string of lights.

"Merry Christmas Eve Eve, son. How was the traffic?"

"Not too bad. This is my friend Bree," I said. Dad still didn't turn around.

"Hi mate! About time my son brought a boyfriend home to meet the family. Although, 'Bree' sounds a bit like a girl's name to me."

"That's because I am a girl, mate!" Bree said smiling, affecting a deep, masculine voice. Dad quickly turned and nearly lost his balance. Luckily, I was close enough to grab hold of the ladder and steady it.

"Pay attention, Dad! You'll break your neck!"

"You two go and make yourself comfortable. I have to finish this in time for tonight."

"You gonna win this year, Dad?"

"Probably not, but I'm following all their rules, so they can't complain..."

Every year, my father enters the neighbourhood Christmas Decoration competition. Spearheaded by some rule-obsessed busy-body up the road, Dad's attempts at 'artistic expression' have been repeatedly thwarted for reasons of safety, coherence, or just plain good taste. I dare not distract Dad by asking what this year's 'masterpiece' consists of. I guess I'll find out at sundown like everyone else.

Bree and I unpack the car and drag everything inside, leaving everything near the foot of the stairs in the living room. I tell Bree we can take everything upstairs in a little while, that we should first check-in with Mission Control aka my mother.

As we entered the huge, open plan kitchen at the rear of the house, it seemed the usual Christmas craziness had already begun. My mother was racing around the kitchen erratically, tearing open kitchen cabinets at random, searching for something. My Aunt Joss was sitting at the kitchen table, nursing a glass of white wine as she watched on with mild amusement as her older sister appeared to be impersonating a headless chicken.

Kathleen Nolan was a big believer in Christmas. More so, she was a believer in putting together and experiencing the 'perfect' Christmas. Whatever the hell that means.

Every year, as the big day approached, my Mum would become increasingly unbalanced as she attempted to squash anything that had the potential to destroy her vision of perfection. This usually ended up descending into chaos and anarchy as the rest of the family would rebel against her 'Deck The Halls' dictatorship.

"Hi Mum," I said as she dashed past me, "What are you looking for?"

"Cake forks!" Mum said with her head under the kitchen sink, "Have you seen them?"

"Well, I've been here for all of three seconds, so no."

"Don't be sarcastic, Charlie. It's Jesus' birthday."

"Not for a couple more days, it isn't. Jesus will have to live with it. Also, aren't we atheists?"

"Did you steal my cake forks?" Mum looked at me with intense scrutiny. I decided to dodge this particular question.

"I'm not even going to dignify that with a response."

"Well, if we don't have cake forks, there won't be any Christmas Cake." Mum pronounced as if she had declared the end of days were here.

"You've never made a Christmas Cake before." Joss chimed in.

"Well I can't if I don't have any cake forks, now can I?"

"We can eat cake without cake forks, Mum!" I said, then wondering why I was involving myself in this conversation.

"Sure, and perhaps I could put the entire Christmas menu in a giant blender and the whole family can eat it out of a trough!"

"It would save on doing the washing up afterward," Joss said mildly, her eye's gleaming knowing that this comment will trigger anything but a mild reaction from her sister.

"I want us to have a nice, normal, family Christmas. Just once. Is that really so much to ask?" Mum said with exasperation.

"And a lack of cake forks is what's stopping us from having that?" I asked, trying and failing to see my mother's point of view.

"Look, those cake forks were antique. They're the only thing that dreadful mother-in-law of mine gave me that was half decent, aside from her dropping dead."

"I bet Jesus loved that comment..." Bree muttered under her breath quietly, but not quietly enough. Mum stopped in her tracks and zeroed in on the outsider.

"Who's this?"

"Mum, this is Bree. Bree, this is my mother Kathleen, and her sister Joss."

Bree smiled and shook hands with Joss. When she offered her hand to Mum, she was awkwardly left hanging as Mum's judgmental eyes scanned my best friend – taking note of the tattoos and ripped jeans. Mum redirected her attention to me.

"Is this why you were fussing on the phone when I asked if you were seeing anyone at the moment?"

I was a little confused. What the hell was Mum on about now?

"Look, I know you haven't had much luck with men, Charlie, but stick with what you know. Besides, I didn't spend all that money on pride flags for your Coming Out party when you were twelve just so my only gay son can throw his life away on some grungy motorcycle moll!"

Bree and I looked at each other and were momentarily stunned. I can honestly say, when I agreed to bring my best friend over as a guest for Christmas, I considered the many ways this action could go horribly wrong. My mother objecting because she was concerned her baby boy was being tempted away from his homosexuality was not one of them. This was too good an opportunity to pass up.

"Did she just call me a moll?" Bree said, trying and failing to hold back her laughter. Despite my mother's outburst, my friend appeared to be having a whale of a time. Perhaps she was finally starting to realise I hadn't been exaggerating all these years.

"Well, Mum," I said, affecting a super deep, super masculine voice, "What can I say? I saw this fine filly at work one day and thought 'Damn, I can't wait to...um... have sex inside her vagina!'"

Is it obvious that I have no experience with seducing women?

"What!?!" My Mum squawked. My Aunt Joss laughed wine through her nose and started coughing. Bree, catching on without a moment's hesitation, grabbed hold of me and started nibbling on my neck in a growling, predatory fashion. Bree started grinding up against me in a display that shocked even me.

"Having sex in my vagina is my favourite kind of sex!" Bree cried.

"Oh, how I love the feeling of your lady parts against me!" I groaned as my father walked into the kitchen, clearly confused by the tableau currently on display.

"Kevin! Do something! Our son is having sex with a girl!" Mum wailed.

"Well, dear. He's our son and we love him. We should support him no matter what. Even it is utterly revolting to witness..." Dad said, grimacing at the sight of Bree snacking on my jugular.

Bree and I couldn't hold back anymore, and we separated and burst out laughing, tears in our eyes.

"You mean, Bree isn't your girlfriend?" Mum said, baffled.

"No! She's just my friend."

"Oh, thank god!" Mum gasped with relief.

"Okay, trying not to take that too personally," Bree muttered.

Mum immediately crossed the kitchen and embraced Bree in a tight hug, "No offense dear, it's just... oh, I'll explain later. Why don't you two settle in, while I try to find these bastard cake forks."

"Forget about the cake forks, Mum. We don't need them!" I said.

"The more you try to get me to forget about them, the more suspicious I become that you're the one who stole them."

I led Bree away from the crazy lady and we gathered our luggage. As we reached the top of the stairs and reached my old bedroom, Bree whispered in my ear.

"Did you steal her cake forks?"

"Not exactly..." I said, not wanting to commit one way or the other to my misdeed.

"You're pure evil!" She said under her breath.

"I learned from the best."

The sleeping arrangements were the same every year. Mum and Dad in their room. Me in mine. Since most of the family lived locally, they would travel to and from their own homes each day. The two other bedrooms, usually occupied by my siblings, were being left intentionally vacant this year in case any of the family has too much to drink and can't drive home. Out in the backyard, next to the pool, is a small two-bedroom guest house. This will be occupied by Aunt Joss and her husband Jack, and my Grandmother, Flo, along with whatever fiance du jour she decides to bring with her.

Bree pulled out the small trundle bed from under my bed and, after a few test bounces, declares it comfortable to sleep on. After putting our luggage away as best we could, we both headed downstairs and out into the garden.

The long covered patio area was already set up with a table big enough for the whole family to gather around. Twinkle lights had been threaded through the roof trusses and support beams. By nightfall, the area should look lovely. Over by the pool, I spotted my Uncle Jack trimming a hedge. He was dressed in an over-the-top Elf costume – the kind you would expect someone to wear if they were working alongside a mall Santa.

Jack was one of those weird people who not only enjoyed Christmas but literally lived for it. He briefly tried to campaign for the family to celebrate Christmas in July as well, but was angrily repulsed.

"Charlie-boy!" Jack called out as we approached. Bree broke away to look at the large flowerbeds my father had carefully put together.

"Hi, Uncle Jack. Merry Christmas."

"Merry Christmas to you, too!" Jack continued on with his hedge trimming.

Jack was lovely, but except for seeing him at Christmas, I had little-to-no-relationship with him. This meant that every year, our interactions would go one of two ways: Either we would have the awkward small talk of two strangers in a lift or the awkward small talk of two strangers in a bar at last call.

"So, Charlie..." Jack said cautiously, clearly trying to come up with something to say, "Are you... still gay?"

A million and one gay jokes whizzed through my mind, and because my brain is totally unfiltered, I smirked and said "Why? Are you offering, Uncle Jack?" punctuating the sentence with a suggestive waggle of my eyebrows.

"Kathleen!" Jack called out, "Your son is trying to molest me!"

From the kitchen window, I heard my mother's voice call out "Charlie, stop molesting your Uncle!"

"Alright, I'll just go and molest my girlfriend then!" I called out, looking at Bree who was watching this bizarre exchange from the other side of the garden with great amusement. After a short silence from the kitchen, my mother replied with "Jack, you do whatever Charlie tells you to do."

I crowed with victory in this... whatever the hell this was. Uncle Jack looked deeply uncomfortable and resumed his trimming, the little bells on his feet and hat sweetly jingling as he moved. I decided I'd teased the poor man enough, so I left him to it.

I caught up with Bree and she asked me about what to expect over the next few days.

"Well, first things first. Always expect the unexpected. You can never anticipate what's going to happen at a Nolan Family Christmas. But as itineraries go, it's basically the same thing every year..."

Christmas Eve Eve is traditionally 'Cocktail Night' where my parents present the family with their latest holiday creation. The evening begins with a light dinner of sausage rolls, fruit mince pies, cabanossi, and little cubes of cheddar cheese, followed by cocktails and drunken debauchery.

Christmas Eve is the infamous Nolan Family Games Night. A different game is played each year, selected by random draw. This is usually the catalyst for fighting, drama, and all-out chaos that overflows into Christmas Day. The family then gathers for lunch on the big day, where the passive aggression and recriminations from Games Night usually boils over into outright hostility.

Finally, a Nolan Family Christmas is concluded with Boxing Day. The day after Christmas is reserved for eating leftovers, licking our wounds, and swearing to all that is holy that we will never do this ever again.

"I can't wait!" Bree said, practically bouncing with excitement. But with the benefit of a lifetime of experience, I know that only bad can come from this. Bree would learn.

Chapter Three – Christmas Eve Eve Pre-Drinks

Pre-Drinks *(definition)*

An Australian tradition of quickly getting drunk at home on cheap alcohol prior to going out for a night on the town, thus saving money on expensive bar prices. This tradition often happens even when the main event is at home, because Australians have a deeply unhealthy relationship with alcohol.

SLOWLY BUT SURELY, the members of the Nolan extended family began trickling in over the course of the latter half of the afternoon. Not just blood relatives, but family friends, people from the neighbourhood and some randoms my parents had invited that nobody seemed to know. It was a running joke in my family that if numbers were looking low, Mum would ring up Rent-A-Crowd.

Within moments of their arrival, each person would be pouring themselves a drink and settling in for the long haul. As dusk approached, it looked like everyone had arrived and was gathered around the big table on the patio.

Bree and I sat together at the far end of the table, watching as my family began to arrive and slowly pickle themselves on everything from slabs of beer that they brought from home, or one of several cheap cask wines that Mum had supplied in an ice-filled Esky near the kitchen door.

The table was covered in plates and platters. All the standard Aussie party foods were represented. Cubed cheddar cheese; chopped up cabanossi; bowls of salted crackers; a crusty cob loaf filled with warm spinach dip; platters of sausage rolls, party pies and, of course, cocktail frankfurts with bowls of tomato dipping sauce. But the biggest platter of all was my Uncle Perry's contribution – a massive pile of homemade fruit mince pies. Perry, my father's brother, brought his hand made creations every year, and every year it was the same. They looked gorgeous with their golden, glazed puff pastry and sweet, spicy, fruity aroma. But beneath the surface lay a danger more terrible than any chemical weapon outlawed by the United Nations.

As Bree reached for one of the fruit mince pies, I quickly slapped her hand and she recoiled.

"Don't eat the fruit mince pies!" I said gravely but sternly.

"Why?" Bree asked, nursing her hand.

"Trust me. They look amazing, but their like a siren's song. Get too close and they'll make you crash onto the rocks..."

"What the hell does that mean?"

"Go over to the platter and listen carefully," I said as a confused Bree got up and bent down over the mountain of pies. She reacted almost immediately.

"What is that? Are they... are they hissing?"

"Hissing? Fizzing? No one is really sure. Either way, there is some kind of ongoing exothermic chemical process going on there that should absolutely never be introduced to a human digestive system."

Bree backed away slowly from the platter of pies, electing to snack on a sausage roll instead. As she raised the baked treat to her mouth, she looked at me, as if silently checking if her selection was safe. I nodded my approval.

"Every year my Uncle Perry makes them, and every year they are a crime against humanity. But despite the entire family knowing the dangers, there's always some idiot who gets drunk and forgets. They end up spending the rest of the holidays in hospital on a stomach pump."

Considering the hell that is a standard Nolan Family Christmas, I briefly gave serious thought to grabbing one of the murder pies and putting an end to it all right here and now. It would no doubt be less painful, but I didn't want to leave Bree alone with this pack of lunatics.

Looking around the table it seemed like everyone was here. Perry was sitting at the other end of the table with his son, Josh. My cousin was busy demolishing a bowl of cocktail frankfurts. As a junior bodybuilder, he was obsessed with protein and other such nonsense. He was also allergic to wearing a shirt. No matter the season, Josh was always 'boiling' and constantly tearing off his shirt. I suspect he was just using it as an excuse to show off his remarkably buff body. Although that didn't explain why he felt the need to disrobe in the middle of our Grandfather's funeral a few years ago.

Flo, my maternal Grandmother was seated at the head of the table next to her new fiance – a tanned, muscular surfy dude wearing a revealing muscle shirt that showed off his impressive chest and abdomen. Drew, who couldn't be more than twenty-five years old, held my Grandmother's hand lovingly while my mother looked on in utter disgust. Flo brings a new, young 'fiance' every Christmas. I wish I knew her secret.

"Would you like another drink, Florence?" Drew said with a deep, husky voice.

"Not right now, lover. Maybe later!" she giggled like a schoolgirl, then winked at the younger man.

"Damn, that Drew guy is hot!" Bree whispers to me. Her opinion quickly changed when, as if on queue, Grandma removed her false teeth, deposited them on the plate in front of her, and she and Drew began open-mouth kissing in a revolting display that was very much not in keeping with the spirit of the season. It looked like something out of a nature documentary about slugs mating. Bree and I turned away from the disturbing public display of affection.

"Mother!" my Mum shrieked at the horrifying display. Flo broke the kiss and turned to her daughter.

"Oh, lighten up, Kathleen! When did you become such a prude, anyway? I remember you pashing on with lots of young men when you were a girl!" the old woman cackled.

"What?" my Dad said sharply, "When was this? And who with? You told me you'd never made out with anyone before!"

"Thanks a lot, Mother!"

Flo just continued to cackle while nonchalantly fondling Drew's muscular thigh. The young man just smiled and whispered something salacious in Flo's ear which had my Grandmother giggling like a schoolgirl again.

Mum and Dad eventually sat down next to Joss and Jack, rounding off what appeared to be the complete guest list. Despite having quite a full house, the absence of my siblings this year did make things seem quieter than usual. Although, I suspected this would not result in a quieter, less chaotic Christmas. Somehow my family, like the universe, always finds a way to course-correct itself.

As the sun set and sky turned into an opal blanket of twinkling stars and swirls of colour, Mum turned on the twinkle lights that had been set up around the patio. Despite having used at least a billion lights, the effect was actually subtle and quite pretty. The same would not be said of my father's creation out the front of the house.

"Alright everyone," Mum announced, "If you'd like to make your way out to the front yard. Kevin is ready to show off this year's Christmas light display!"

Bree and I followed as the family filed out of the patio via the side gate and made our way to the front lawn. Several of the other houses had their displays switched on, bathing the neighbourhood in a warm background light. Everyone gathered around as Dad held up two electrical cords dramatically. I quietly pulled out two pairs of sunglasses from my back pocket and handed one to Bree. When she looked at me questioningly, I just mouthed the words "Trust me" to her. We put on the sunglasses and watched on as Dad snapped together the two cords.

The area was suddenly enveloped by an odd, electrical buzzing noise. The kind of thing you would hear in a mad scientist's laboratory in an old science fiction movie. Seconds later, we were hit by a sudden flash of light. The whole front of the house was a blinding wall of light that burned brighter than the sun. The street went from night to day. Our family shielded their eyes as Bree and I watched on. Although the sunglasses didn't offer perfect protection, they allowed me to make out at least part of my father's display. The roof had a massive banner message written in lights. The words 'Something Simple' would be burned into the corneas of any poor unsuspecting passerby.

"Something Simple? What does that mean, Dad?" I asked.

"That old busybody up the street who runs the contest told me to just do 'something simple' this year – so I did." he said with an evil grin.

My Dad, the king of malicious compliance.

Once the majority of the family had regained their eyesight, we returned, stumbling, back to the patio and resumed our places around the big table. It was at this point the Pre-Drinks portion of the night really kicked in. Bree and I held back, nursing our white wines, as neither of us are big drinkers, while the rest of the family rapidly downed drink after drink.

It wasn't long before the family started splitting into groups. The men gathered together and began arguing over which was more festive: party pies or mini sausage rolls. The women gathered together and began scathingly bitching about relatives and friends who were unable to attend this year. All the while, Mum was buzzing around making sure plates were full, glasses were freshened and everything was going 'smoothly' as she liked to refer to it.

The doorbell rang, and I got up to answer it. But before I knew what was happening, my mother damn-near crash-tackled me, insisting that she would answer the door. I immediately start seeing red flags.

She's up to something.

It's then I remember Mum asking all sorts of questions a few days ago, and realising that the new arrival is almost certainly my 'blind date' for the evening.

When I tell Bree that I'm about to be pimped out to some total stranger, she giggles and begins bouncing with excitement. I wanted to smack her one. I idly wondered which secretly straight man Mum has managed to recruited this year, but as she returned to the patio with a wide smile on her face, a tall man following in her wake, my heart froze and my lungs deflated.

No way. No fucking way.

She can't have done this.

I'm going to kill her.

"Everyone!" my soon-to-be-deceased Mum announced to the assembled masses, "May I introduce our surprise Christmas guest. Charlie's old friend, Liam!"

Liam, who I hadn't seen in eight years. Liam, who was more handsome than ever. Liam, who shattered my heart into a million pieces.

The family cheered and welcomed Liam.

I wanted to die.

Chapter Four – Blast From The Past

IT TOOK EVERYTHING within me to maintain my composure as I watched Liam do the rounds, shaking hands with members of my family and exchanging pleasantries.

What the hell was my mother thinking?

Why had she invited the one man who had torn out my heart and trampled on it until it was a bloody pulp? The obvious answer was that she clearly *wasn't t*hinking. Mum had apparently lost her mind and I now had all the evidence I needed to have her locked up forever in that dodgy mental hospital I saw on the news last week.

"Are you okay?" Bree asked gently, stroking my arm in an attempt to comfort me. But no amount of arm stroking was going to dissipate the white-hot rage that was boiling up inside me. I was filled with so much anger, I could conceivably use it to fly a space shuttle to the moon. But, being the man I am, not wanting to make a fuss or spark yet another Nolan family drama, I did what I always did.

I repressed my true feelings.

"I'm fine," I said softly.

I took a couple of deep breaths, calmed myself and then stood up, hoping to melt into the crowd. At this point, my best bet was to try and avoid Liam for as long as possible. I might be able to repress feelings from a distance, but I couldn't guarantee it if I had to actually interact with him up close. As for my mother, well, she is the deadest dead woman in Deadonia.

Alas, my avoidance plan was doomed to failure. Kathleen, having proudly paraded her latest matchmaking achievement around the rest of the family, had taken Liam by the arm and was now guiding him my way.

Fuck.

My mother was smiling like a Cheshire cat; smug and genuinely proud of herself. She clearly had no idea how much she had fucked up. Given that I never shared the full details of why Liam and I ended our relationship, that was probably to be expected. But what the hell was she doing interfering in my personal life in the first place? And why in the name of all that is holy would she think it was a good idea to fix me up with the only ex-boyfriend I'd ever introduced her to?

'...They're coming to take her away – Haha!'

"Sweetheart!" the dead woman said cheerily, "You remember Liam, of course, and Liam – this is Charlie's friend, Bree."

Liam smiled and offered a hand to Bree. Bree scowled at him, took his hand and crushed it in her surprisingly strong, vice-like grip. Liam somehow managed to avoid whimpering, despite the audible sound of bones popping and clicking. I managed to suppress my smirk at that.

Bree was fucking awesome sometimes.

"Yes, yes I think I do remember Liam. Long time no see." I said neutrally.

Liam, to his credit, looked slightly uncomfortable. He made no attempt to shake my hand. He was probably afraid I would tear it off.

"Well, I'll let you kids mingle. Time to get to work on the cocktails!" Mum said, dashing away into the crowd.

"You're looking good Charlie. Time has been kind to you," he said with a smile, oozing confidence. It was almost like the last eight years hadn't happened.

"Thanks. You too."

Why am I returning his compliment? Sure, time had been kind to him. In the eight years since I last saw him, very little of Liam's already handsome features had been diminished. In fact, most of them had been refined. His warm, tanned skin and dark chocolate brown eyes were as captivating as ever; His dark hair, once spiky and messy, was now thick and soft-looking; His beautiful facial structure was now enhanced by a carefully maintained crop of designer stubble.

Where once upon a time, Liam had looked a bit like a scruffy skateboarder, now he looked like a polished GQ model. But the fact that he looked amazing was irrelevant. This wasn't a blind date. This wasn't a date of any kind. This was me randomly bumping into my ex at a party. My cheating ex. My cheating ex who broke my heart. I needed to remember that.

"Well, it was nice seeing you again, Liam. If you'll excuse us..." I grabbed Bree's arm and I none-to-subtly dragged her away. Like the loyal friend she was, she never once broke eye contact with Liam, scowling the whole time. Liam, on the other hand, went from a confident smile to looking sombre. His eyes, which had been bright a few moments ago, were now flat and dull like he was disappointed for some reason.

I ended up dragging Bree around the side of the house, away from the rest of the family and prying eyes.

"If I ask you if you're okay now, are you gonna tell me you're fine again?" Bree asked, sensing I was moments from falling apart.

I couldn't even summon up the energy to respond. Bree opened her arms, and I entered embrace instinctively. I couldn't hold it back anymore, and I silently sobbed into my friend's hair. She just rubbed my back in soothing circles and let me have my moment. When I regained my composure, I gave her a slight squeeze and Bree released me from the hug.

"I'm sorry," I said in a whisper, "I don't know what came over me."

"You were hurting and you needed to let it out. It's nothing to be ashamed of."

"It's my family. They're a bad influence. I never react like this except when I'm around them. But I was totally blindsided by this. What the hell is my Mum playing at? Inviting Liam to Christmas? Has she lost her fucking mind?"

"No idea. Surely she knows he's your ex?" Bree asked.

"Of course. I never told my family the details of the breakup. I didn't want to stir up drama. I just told them 'things didn't work out' and that was that."

"Even still, you'd think your Mum would check with you before inviting someone like an ex."

"Mum isn't known for doing what the average person would expect."

"Well, what's the plan now? Do you want to leave?"

"More than anything," I said to Bree, "But nothing short of death will get me a 'get out of jail free' card. But I am definitely going to have a word with my mother. I need to know what the hell she is up to."

Bree returned to the patio while I quietly slipped inside the house and headed for the kitchen. Mum and Dad were busy prepping large jugs of whatever monstrous cocktails they had devised for the party. Mum spotted me and gave me a massive smile which died on her lips the moment she saw the look on my face.

"Darling, is everything okay?"

"Burial or cremation?"

"I beg your pardon?" Mum said with a slight stutter.

"Which would you prefer? Because you are so massively dead!" I said, my voice cold and low.

"Charlie, your father and I have to get these cocktails finished and..."

"What the hell are you doing, Mum? Why did you invite Liam? How did you even get into contact with him? Why is he here?"

I was doing everything I could to remain calm, but that white-hot rage was quickly boiling up within me again, and if I wasn't careful, my mother would soon get to witness my eerily accurate impression of Krakatoa.

"I ran into him in the city a couple of weeks ago. I was out for the day shopping and just bumped into him. We got to chatting and he told me how much he misses you and would love to catch up with you again. So I told him he was welcome to spend Christmas with us and catch up on old times with you."

"WHY?" I said sharply, so sharply that my father almost dropped the bottle of vodka in his hand.

"He was always such a lovely boy. I never did understand why things never worked out between you. God knows you've never found anyone better since. Plus, he was always a looker, but now? Phwoar!"

"Kathleen!" Dad said, not appreciating his wife's tone.

"Oh please, Kevin. You'd root him too given half the chance!"

"He is handsome, I'll give you that. But I don't need you going all gaga over him, woman. I should be more than enough for you!"

"Oh, you are, my gorgeous husband. You truly are. And if you find the plastic mistletoe, I may just show you how much you mean to me..."

"Um hello? I'm still here, you two!" I said indignantly.

"Not now Charlie, Your father and I need to get these cocktails out, then I'm going to let your father unwrap one of his presents early!" Mum said with a salacious wink.

"Gross!"

Mum and Dad grabbed the huge jugs of cocktails and started heading out to the patio, effectively ending the conversation. Not knowing what else to do, I followed in their wake and rejoined Bree at the table.

"Everyone!" my Mum announced loudly, "Everyone please return to the table. Cocktail Night is about to begin!"

The family started slowly making their way back to their places at the table, with Liam taking a seat at the opposite end of the table. It was going to take more than a couple of my parent's dodgy cocktails to get through this night. I lamented the lost opportunity to have blatted myself with one of Uncle Perry's fruit mince pies. The way this weekend was shaping up, a couple of nights in hospital on a stomach pump was looking better and better by the moment.

Chapter Five – Cocktails and Chaos

BEING A WARM, humid night in the height of the Australian Summer, it, of course, made perfect sense for my entire family to gather on the patio for Cocktail Night, rather than experience the cool, air-conditioned comfort of the enormous downstairs rumpus room. My mother was a master of cruelty.

The rumpus room, as per usual, was off-limits to everyone until Christmas Day. First thing on Christmas morning, everyone would be allowed downstairs to exchange and open gifts, eat Christmas lunch at the big table that Mum will have spent several days setting up with all the good plates and glassware. Eventually, the whole family will gather around downstairs to engage in bare-knuckle fist fighting or possibly some kind of knife fight. Well, at least, some shouting and screaming at each other as is traditional in a Nolan Family Christmas.

But for now, we were stuck outside in the balmy humidity, preparing to be dazzled by my parent's latest alcoholic creation. In what could only be described as some kind of failure of pack mentality, I appeared to be the only one who remembers how awful these bloody cocktails are every year. For some reason, everyone else looked genuinely excited as Mum and Dad brought out jug after jug of some noxious-looking substance along with a couple of trays filled with empty glass tumblers.

Back in the early 1990s, my parents went on a one-day cocktail making course at the local pub. Ever since the pair of them have been convinced that they are boutique artisan bartenders. Each Christmas, they put their heads together and try to come up with a new and amazing cocktail to share with the family. Each year, they fail miserably and end up creating some crime against humanity that leaves their family in a crumpled, broken mess on the floor.

Last year's entry, the now infamous 'Reindeer Bright' cocktail, was a putrid green concoction that was liberally garnished with red glace cherries. The full horror of my parent's creation was not revealed until the following morning when, one by one, each member of the family discovered the revolting drink had turned their bowel movements fluorescent green.

Yet despite this, everyone appeared to be keen to try their latest experiment. Even Bree, thrill seeker that she was, looked like she was willing to throw caution to the wind and give it a try.

Silly rabbit.

Over the years, I had perfected the art of avoidance when it came to the annual Cocktail Night. My strategy was deceptively simple. I just made sure I always had a near-full drink in my hand at all times. That way, when my parents tried to offer me a refill, they wouldn't have a chance. Usually, I would already have helped myself to a glass of scotch, but the run-in with Liam had thrown me out of schedule. I was now drinkless and open to attack. No problem though, I'll just accept one of the putrid cocktails and nurse it for the rest of the night.

Speaking of the devil drink, I watched on as my parents started pouring glass after glass of their latest creation. A thick, creamy white, slightly chunky concoction with a similar consistency to a smoothie. I dared not ask what the ingredients were.

"Well, Everyone!" Mum announced, "Here it is! This year's special cocktail – our 'Tropical Snowball!'"

Everyone cheered and applauded. I'll give Mum credit where credit was due – she was quite the showman and knew how to work a crowd.

"Believe it or not, we didn't actually invent the cocktail this year…" Mum continued, sparking my attention, "but adapted it from the Gay and Lesbian Alliance Against Defamation's Cocktail Book. We gave it a different name though because the original name wasn't very festive."

Who knew GLAAD made a cocktail book? I guess you learn something new every day. Well, since my parents didn't invent this cocktail, maybe it won't be so bad?

That's gotta be wishful thinking.

Mum and Dad started making the rounds, handing out tall glasses of Tropical Snowballs and the overwhelming reaction appeared to be positive. That being said, my family would react positively if my parents were handing out tall, frosty glasses of battery acid. When they finally made their way around to us, Bree immediately grabbed a glass and took a long healthy swig of the mysterious liquid. I held my breath as I watched her swallow, mentally preparing myself to drive her to the emergency room if needed.

My parents were also waiting with bated breath for Bree's verdict. The family would be expected to be polite and be positive about their creation, but a virtual stranger's opinion was likely to be more honest.

"Oh my god..." Bree said, drawing out her reply, "It's really... really good!"

I quirked my eyebrows at her, silently asking her if she was entirely serious, but she simply took another sip and reiterated how much she liked the cocktail. I was genuinely aghast. Maybe the impossible had finally happened. Perhaps I was actually witnessing a real-life Christmas miracle. Had my parents actually managed to put together a cocktail that was not only tasty but non-lethal?

"Go, on Charlie. Try it!" Bree encouraged, taking another glass of my mother's tray and foisting it upon me. I was still a little wary.

"What was the original name of this cocktail, again?" I asked Mum.

"I told you, darling. It wasn't very festive, that's why we changed it," she said quietly, apparently trying not to draw attention to this topic of conversation.

"But what was it called?"

"It doesn't matter." Mum's toned suggested she was quickly becoming frustrated.

"If it doesn't matter, why don't you just tell me?"

"A Cum Bucket!" Mum cried out, "It was called a Cum Bucket! Are you happy now?"

Silence befell the patio as the entire family stopped what they were doing and turned to stare, open-mouthed, at my mother's sudden outburst. After a few moments, my grandmother started laughing like a witch, which set off everyone else. My Mum's face flushed with embarrassment and she dashed away into the kitchen, abandoning the half-empty tray of cocktails on the table.

Dad held back as long as he could, but even he couldn't help laughing. He abandoned his tray of cocktails as well, then followed his wife inside the house, no doubt to try and calm her down.

"Well, are you going to drink it or not?" Bree asked, polishing off her glass and picking up another from one of the discarded trays.

"I dunno…"

"Charlie," Bree held the glass up to my lips like she were about to feed a child with the old 'here comes the aeroplane' routine, "take a little sip for me."

"Get away from me, madwoman!"

"C'mon, drink Mummy's Cum Bucket!" She said with a wicked grin on her face.

"You are revolting!" I said incredulously.

"And you're a big prude. Drink the fucking cocktail and stop being such a big nancy boy. I'm your girlfriend. I command you!"

"Really? One of my parent's cocktails and you're already name-calling? Pfft! Lightweight! And as for girlfriend, consider yourself officially dumped!"

"Get it up ya!" Bree cheered, and for the sake of shutting her up, I picked up the glass and took a small sip.

I was genuinely surprised at how good it actually tasted. Creamy and sweet, with the distinct flavours of banana, pineapple and coconut.

It didn't have much of an alcoholic taste. Bree cheered again as I took another, more substantial sip of the cocktail.

Before I knew it, the glass was empty and I was pleasantly surprised that I was feeling well, with no deleterious side effects. I didn't even feel drunk. Maybe the cocktail didn't have much alcohol in it? Maybe my parents had discovered what a 'mocktail' was and decided to experiment? Who knows? But when Mum and Dad returned to the patio, and the whole family erupted in cheers of congratulations. Dad kissed Mum on the cheek, and she blushed brightly at all the adulation for their cocktail. Bree and I knocked back another glass each and joined in on the animated conversations that were going on around us.

~

Within an hour or so, my whole family was ridiculously drunk. Grandma Flo was singing show tunes in the corner. Aunt Joss was dancing with a potted pine tree. My Cousin Josh was shirtless and pole-dancing in what appeared to be some kind of drunken homage to Magic Mike. Bree was drinking more cocktails and I was feeling great. I wasn't even concerned about Liam, who was sitting at the other end of the table looking at me. Everyone else was laughing a lot and telling each other stories. All things considered, everything was going really well.

Too well.

By the pricking of my thumbs, something wicked this way comes...

I knew from past experience that a Nolan Family Christmas doesn't go this smoothly without the universe serving out something super nasty to counterbalance things. But at that exact moment, all I could care about was going to the bathroom. The cocktails were delicious, but like any alcoholic drinks - you never buy them, only rent them.

As I went to stand up, I suddenly realised my legs were not working properly. I felt perfectly sober, but my legs felt like I'd been binge drinking since dawn. I managed to stand, but my wobbly pins were quickly spreading their incapacity upwards. Like getting drunk backwards.

What the hell was in those cocktails?

I couldn't focus on people or conversations. Everything was in flux, making it difficult to know where I was going. All I cared about was getting inside to the bathroom so I could pee. I stumbled through the sliding patio door and managed to grip the wall. I carefully made my way down the corridor and around the corner before stumbling into the downstairs bathroom. I quickly took care of business and washed my hands, all while trying to avoid looking in the mirror. I didn't want to know what I looked like.

How did I let myself get this drunk? I never get this drunk.

When I opened the bathroom door and stepped out, I saw Liam standing there, his face a study of concern.

"Charlie, are you okay? You look a little unsteady?"

My head was spinning. I didn't know which way was up. The last thing I saw was the floor suddenly flying at me, then sinking into a dark pool of blackness.

Chapter Six – The Morning After

I SLOWLY AWOKE from my drunken stupor through a haze of pain and misery the likes of which I have never experienced in my entire life. Unlike the rest of my family, I have never been a big drinker. Hangovers were never a problem for me – until now.

I don't understand how I got so mind-numbingly drunk. I only had two drinks last night. I know I'm not much of a drinker, but I've never been that much of a lightweight. My skull felt like it was fractured and my brain was an oozing puddle of goo. When I stupidly attempted to open my eyes, the gentle beams of early morning light streaming in through the nearby window were like razor blades on my retinas. My stomach churned, my throat was dry and my mouth felt like it had been scrubbed out with sandpaper. All in all – I was not feeling my best.

All this focus on my physical condition was probably the reason why I hadn't bothered to ask myself where I was. The last clear memory I had was leaving the patio to find the bathroom. Even without opening my eyes, I knew I was in a bed. I was wearing only my underwear. I was covered by one of my Mum's gloriously soft and comfortable doona quilts. The room was silent, except for what sounded like running water coming from the next room.

A shower?

I dared to open my eyes again, and this time I was able to focus a bit better without being blinded by the soft sunlight. After a few moments, I realised I was not in my bedroom. I was in my brother's room. I was alone in bed.

I must have been really drunk last night. I fell asleep in the wrong bedroom!

The running water sound stopped, and I looked toward the closed door of the ensuite bathroom. I did my best to sit up in bed, my stomach and head still protesting this much activity. Obviously, Bree must have found me and joined me in here. But why didn't she just sleep in my room? I was pretty sure there wasn't a trundle bed in my brother's room.

The bathroom door opened and out stepped Liam. He was naked with the exception of a small bath towel wrapped around his waist. His hair was damp and slicked back. His skin, moist and steaming in the cool morning air. His body was very different from the last time I saw him like this. He was always attractive, but it was clear that Liam had spent almost every day of the last eight years working out at his local gym. His lightly defined features had been developed and enhanced. His pecs, abs and obliques looked as if they had been carved out of the richest Italian marble. His light sprinkling of body hair, looking darker after showering, only served to heighten his physique.

If I didn't feel like I'd just been fed through a meat grinder, I would be drooling at this early morning vision. But there were two slight problems. Firstly, what the hell was I doing here with Liam? And secondly, no matter how delicious his body looked, this was still the man who broke my heart. I needed to keep that in my badly hungover mind. I sagged back down on the pillows beneath me and hoped the mattress would swallow me whole.

"Morning sleepyhead," Liam said softly with a smile, "How are you feeling?"

"Like someone dropped the Hubble telescope on my head." I groaned.

"There's a glass of chilled water and some headache tablets on the bedside table. I thought you might need them."

I looked to my side and, sure enough, there sat a tall glass of water and some tablets. I swallowed them and carefully drank the water. The cool liquid was like a panacea. Within moments, my stomach stopped churning and my mouth and throat were feeling much better. Hopefully, my headache would calm down shortly too. Unfortunately, nothing would make the rest of this situation better.

"What happened to my clothes?"

"I took them off when I put you to bed. You were, well, a little messy." Liam said, trying to be delicate.

Oh, God. Did I puke all over myself? Gross...

"Oh, wow. Thanks. So, you and I... we didn't..."

Liam's eyebrows knitted together in a frown I'd long forgotten.

"No, we didn't have sex, Charlie." he said coldly, "You were unconscious. No matter how low your opinion of me, I can't believe you'd think I was capable of that."

I immediately felt ashamed. He was correct. I could lay a lot at his door, but Liam was not the kind of man to take advantage of someone who had had too much to drink.

"I'm sorry. That was a stupid thing to ask. My head is still messed up. I don't know what happened. The last thing I remember was trying to get to the bathroom."

Liam's features relaxed. He sat down on the edge of the bed and held my hand.

"I found you outside the bathroom. You could barely stand. You collapsed and puked everywhere. I cleaned you up as best I could and took you upstairs. I wasn't sure which room you were staying in, so I thought it best to take you to my room so I could keep an eye on you."

I blushed, embarrassment flooding me. Taking pity on me, Liam gently patted my hand and smiled.

"Why don't you go and have a shower? I bet the hot water will make you feel a thousand times better."

I nodded and disentangled myself carefully from the bedcovers. As I did, Liam stood, turned away and dropped the towel. He retrieved a fresh pair of underpants from the dresser in front of him and put them on.

Some things never change. Liam was never one to be bashful.

"Thanks. For looking after me. I'm not sure I deserve it."

"Oh, I dunno. Something tells me you don't make a habit of binge drinking."

"Definitely not. I'm not even sure that's what I did last night. God knows what was in those cocktails."

I headed into the bathroom and Liam was right. The hot water and steam was nothing short of heavenly. All the aches in my muscles and the feelings of nausea slowly started to ebb away. By the time I got out of the shower and dried myself, my headache had reduced to a dull throb. I tied a towel around my waist and returned to the bedroom to find Liam fully dressed and reading something on a Kindle. Liam was always an avid reader.

"Better?" he asked, looking up and smiling.

"Much. I'll just go get some clothes from next door. Then we can go scrounge up some coffee from downstairs."

Liam nodded and returned to his reading. I stepped out of the room and walked down the hall to my bedroom. I opened the door slowly to find my bed occupied. Bree was out to the world, looking as annihilated as I did a few minutes ago. But beside her was a very humanoid-shaped lump under the bedcovers. From the doorway, I couldn't see who it was. I carefully stepped into the room and retrieved some clothes from one of my bags. I slipped into the bathroom, quickly dressed and brushed my teeth, then stepped quietly back into my bedroom. I was shocked to see the sleeping face of the bed's other occupant: my soon-to-be Grandpa, Drew.

I crept out of the room as quietly as possible and closed the door. I couldn't believe what I had just seen. Nolan Family Christmases were known for their soap opera-like drama, but this was a plot twist nobody saw coming.

~

Liam and I descended the stairs to the living room, which now looked more like a makeshift morgue. It would seem I was not the only one to be destroyed by a certain festive drink last night. It seemed most of my family were camped out on the living room floor in a crumpled heap. Mild groaning could be heard emanating from the pitiful group as we tip-toed passed them into the kitchen.

I was feeling better than I had, but the bright, morning light streaming through the big kitchen windows almost killed me on the spot. I squinted until my rattled brain adapted. Mum was busy working on cooking breakfast for the hungover masses, while Dad was furiously reading what appeared to be some kind of legal document. I couldn't help noticing that neither of my parents appeared to be in any way worse for wear.

"Morning, Dad," I said to my father, who looked up briefly and grunted.

"Your father got a 'cease-and-desist' letter from the council this morning. Apparently, his Christmas lights display is a violation of EPA guidelines or something," Mum said as she stirred a pan of scrambled eggs.

"I'm sorry," my Dad said venomously to nobody in particular, "I thought we lived in Australia, not Stalin's Russia!"

"Stalin had strong opinions on Christmas lights?" I asked, my muddled brain not quite following the conversation.

"Next they'll be coming into our homes in the middle of the night and dragging us off to the gulags!" Dad muttered under his breath as he stared at the offending document, possibly trying to make it burst into flames using only the power of his mind.

"So," I said, trying to change the subject, "Why aren't you two both groaning and in agony like everyone else?"

"Oh, we didn't drink much last night," Mum said brightly, "We were hosting after all. Had to keep on the ball."

I sat down at the kitchen table and grabbed a hold of my head with both hands. Dad mercifully brought over a big mug of coffee with milk and sugar – just the way I like it. I thanked him and sipped the hallowed nectar of the gods. The caffeine almost immediately started rebooting my synapses and my fuzzy hangover head finally started to dissipate. I turned to Liam, who had sat down next to me, and was looking equally as unaffected by the previous evening.

"I assume you didn't drink the cocktail either, since you're also not groaning and begging for death?"

"I couldn't. I'm lactose intolerant, remember?"

Oh, yeah. I'd forgotten about that. Lucky bastard.

"What the hell was in that cocktail, Mum? That thing was lethal!"

"Oh don't be such a wuss!" Mum gently chastised as she continued to cook scrambled eggs on the stove, "We followed the recipe exactly. Who would have thought we would have had so many lightweights in this family?"

It was then I noticed a piece of brightly coloured paper under the fruit bowl on the kitchen table. It appeared to have rainbows on it. I pulled it out and took a closer look. It was a flyer for a gay club in Melbourne. It was advertising a new cocktail and something called 'drag bingo' on Sunday afternoons. Closer examination revealed that this, and not some cocktail book, was the origin of the previous night's cocktail.

"Is this where you got the recipe from?" I held the flyer up to my mother, who smiled and nodded.

"This isn't a cocktail book. And it's certainly not by the GLAAD. Where did you get that idea from?" I asked as I read the flyer, discovering the section on cocktails did actually contain a recipe for the infamous 'Cum Bucket' cocktail.

"Oh, I don't know darling. I skimmed over it. My mind must have filled in the blanks."

"Well, it must have filled in a lot of blanks. I now know why that cocktail was so lethal. It's a shooter!"

My parents, the supposed master bartenders, looked at me blankly.

"It's meant to be served in a shot glass, not a tall tumbler. Each of those cocktails you served last night must have been the equivalent of around twelve standard drinks!"

"Whoops..." Mum eventually said, blushing slightly.

"Whoops? Are you kidding? You give the whole family alcohol poisoning and all you can say is 'Whoops?'"

"What can I say? We didn't have any shot glasses. I just figured everyone would have a few anyway, so why not just serve them in big glasses instead of lots of little small ones."

I rubbed my head again.

"Hang on!" I grabbed the flyer again and scanned it quickly, "This cocktail has three different liqueurs in it. Those cocktails last night must have cost an absolute fortune! Have you lost your minds?"

"It's Christmas!" my parents drawled in unison as if this somehow explained why spending what must have been close to a grand on alcohol, that almost poisoned the entire family, made even the remotest bit of sense.

My family would be the death of me.

Thankfully, Dad came over with plates of bacon, eggs and toast for Liam and I. I was initially queasy at the sight of the greasy mess presented to me, but I forced myself to eat it and found it did me the world of good.

The smell of bacon must have woken up the army of darkness in the living room, as my extended family started slowly coming through into the kitchen. A destroyed Bree collapsed in the chair next to me and I smiled evilly at her. She gave me a confused look. I mouthed the words "Grandma's gonna kill you!" and her face went white as a sheet. I grinned like the Cheshire Cat at her mortification.

This Christmas, like every Christmas, was going to be another swirling vortex of unpredictable drama and senseless destruction. But on the positive side, no one could accuse it of being boring.

Chapter Seven – Afternoon Recovery

BY LUNCHTIME, MOST of the family who were not staying at the house had recovered enough to drive themselves back to their homes. They needed to clean themselves up, recuperate and possibly sneak in a little nap before they continued into the next ring of hell.

I mean the next night of celebrating.

All of them promised to return that evening for the continuation of the Nolan Family Christmas shenanigans but, to be completely honest, after the chaos of the previous evening I doubt anyone would have blamed them if they all ran for the hills and never came back.

I almost felt sorry for Bree. Even after several cups of coffee and a greasy breakfast that could choke a whale to death, she still looked like she had been hit by a heavy goods truck.

I *almost* felt sorry for her.

I warned her going in that a Nolan Family Christmas was not for the faint of heart and, for the first time since arriving, I think Bree was finally beginning to understand the full depths of my warning. She had yet to summon up enough courage to remove her sunglasses, as she was still suffering from a severe headache, and the less said about her hair the better. Let's just say, she could get a government funding grant if she submitted it as a modern art installation.

I finally managed to convince her to return to bed for a few hours. Some sleep, some headache tablets and perhaps a quick exorcism would do her the world of good. I decided not to cheekily comment on making sure she was *alone* in bed this time because hungover or not, she would kill me stone dead.

After breakfast, I helped Mum and Dad wash up the huge pile of dishes, load up the dishwasher with all the glassware from the previous night and give the kitchen a quick tidy. Afterwards, I felt drained and decided I needed to do a little self-care if I was going to make it through the rest of the day and evening. I found a quiet spot outside in the garden, sat down in the shade and started reading. I brought a couple of books with me, along with my Kindle, but I ended up reading one of Mum's books. It was some murder mystery about a family wedding on an isolated tropical island, where the characters are killed off one-by-one by some mysterious psychopath. As I read, I quietly wondered to myself if it was too late to get a group booking there.

After an hour or so, I was feeling more or less back to normal. But I was still feeling a bit shaken. Not from the cocktails, but from the rest of the evening. I couldn't help but feel enumerably embarrassed from my behaviour the previous night. I never get drunk. I certainly never get drunk to the point of blacking out. While it certainly wasn't entirely my fault (those cocktails should be banned by an act of Parliament) I ultimately had to take responsibility for my own actions. The fact that Liam had been so kind about it all only seemed to make it worse. I didn't want him to be kind. I didn't want him to be anything. I'd had eight years to get him out of my system, yet one act of compassion was all it seemed to take to make me start feeling things again.

No. This was not going to happen. I needed to focus. I needed to be sensible. This was the man who cheated on me. This was the man who broke my heart. This was the man who, when I broke up with him, made no attempt to convince me to stay or even fight for our relationship. He just let me walk away without a second glance.

Whoa! Where did that come from? Did I want him to fight for me?

Those cocktails must have damaged my brain even more than I thought. I needed to focus on what *is* and not what *was*.

Liam and I are ancient history. There are no second chances. Besides, why would I want a second chance with a cheating man-whore who clearly didn't want me anyway?

It was then the peace of my garden sanctuary was obliterated by the one person I really didn't want to see.

"Are you feeling better?" Liam said as he approached casually. He was barefoot and his button-up was undone, revealing his sculpted torso as his shirt flapped in the gentle breeze. The man looked like a Calvin Klein commercial. It just wasn't fair.

"Yeah, I'm all good now." I tried to focus on my book.

"Well, if last night was what your family does as an opening act for Christmas, what comes next?"

"Chemical weapons. Psychological warfare. You never know with this lot."

"So be prepared for anything, huh?" he chuckled.

"What are you doing here, Liam?" I decided not to beat around the bush anymore.

"Your Mum invited me?"

"Eight years after we broke up? Come on..."

"Alright, it wasn't entirely your Mum's doing. I wanted to see you."

"Why?"

"I've gone through a lot of stuff since we broke up. Things have changed in my life. I've changed. But despite all that, I never stopped caring about you, Charlie. Never."

"I've moved on. We both have."

"Why did you break up with me?" Liam asked, his voice soft, almost a whisper. I looked up at his face and I had never seen him look so vulnerable.

"You know why."

"You said things weren't working out, but what did that actually mean. You never said."

"You never asked," I replied acidly.

"You're right. I didn't. That was one of many mistakes that I made. I wish I could go back and change what happened between us."

"It's been eight years, Liam. Does it really matter after all this time?"

"It matters to me. And I was kind of hoping that maybe it mattered to you too."

I'd had enough of this conversation. I was never a confrontational person, and I wasn't sure what Liam's agenda was, but I wasn't going to go raking through the muck of our past. I stood up, shook my head and started to walk away.

"If you want to play games, stick around for tonight. It's our annual Games Night. My family will eat you alive." I said without looking back.

Christmas Eve Games Night was infamous in our family for triggering fights and resentments that would usually boil over spectacularly on Christmas Day. And given the sparks that were already floating in the air, this year's Games Night was shaping up to be more explosive than ever before.

Chapter Eight – Let The Games Begin

I WENT UPSTAIRS to my bedroom to find Bree awake, showered, dressed and looking a lot better than she had done only a few hours earlier. Gone were the bloodshot eyes and sickly complexion, replaced with brightness and vitality. Apparently recovered from her severe hangover, Bree was sitting on the end of the bed, absently brushing her dark hair.

"I see you're looking a bit more human now. Feeling better?"

"Oh God, yes!" she said with confidence, "Nothing a quick nap and a hot shower couldn't cure. Now I'm ready to dive into Games Night. I can't wait, it sounds like fun!"

I rolled my eyes at her unbridled enthusiasm. Seriously, had the cocktail debacle taught her nothing? How was she still excited for this? Why was she not wanting to run for her life?

Then it hit me. She was trying to distract me.

Nice try, dear friend!

"So, last night was... interesting," I say nonchalantly.

"Yeah, you and Liam reconnecting after all these years. How are you feeling about that?"

"Oh no. We aren't talking about that yet. We're talking about you. Specifically, you and a certain someone I found you cosied up to in my bed..."

If my smirk was any wider, it would hurt. I was loving this. Bree was blushing furiously.

"I don't know what happened!" She eventually offered, "One minute, I'm downstairs with everyone having cocktails. The next minute, I'm dragging Drew upstairs with me. The next thing I remember, it's morning and we're cuddled up together in bed. Neither of us could remember doing anything. How could this have happened?"

"My parent's cocktails. They damn near gave everyone alcohol poisoning. I had more or less the same experience with Liam, except he was sober. He put me to bed after I blacked out."

"Please don't tell anyone about me and Drew. I don't think anything actually happened between us, but I can't imagine I'd be welcome if your family found out I spent the night with your Grandmother's fiance."

I mimed a key locking my lips and gave her a big hug.

"Meanwhile, how *are* you feeling about seeing Liam again?"

"I can honestly say it's a mixed bag. I'm still upset about how things ended between us. I'm embarrassed about getting smashed out of my brain and having him, of all people, find me and take care of me. I keep remembering all the good things about him and now every time I see him, it's like this major internal conflict. I can't believe my Mum would invite him for Christmas. She must be out of her mind."

"Maybe," Bree said cautiously, "Maybe not. Sounds to me you still have some feelings for Liam. At the very least, things sound unresolved between the two of you. Maybe now would be a good time, given the benefit of time and perspective, to sort out how you really feel about him. Maybe even confront him about your breakup."

"Oh no. I don't do confrontations. That's the kind of drama my family thrives on."

"That's up to you. But from where I'm standing, you'll never truly get over Liam until you actually sit down and talk to him about what happened between the two of you. If nothing else, it may give you the closure you need so you can finally move on with your life."

Closure. The idea was such a foreign concept to me. In my family, arguments and fights were rarely wrapped up neatly. We would just argue until someone got tired and couldn't be bothered arguing anymore. No one would apologise. No closure would be obtained. The fight would forever remain unresolved.

"Maybe you're right. Maybe I do need to have a talk with him. But honestly, I hope this doesn't turn into another epic Nolan Christmas drama. I don't think I could deal with that. Hopefully, I can corner him somewhere private and have it out quietly away from the others."

Bree smiles and embraces me in another big hug, then returns to brushing her hair.

~

When we go downstairs and out onto the patio, we find that my family has slowly begun gathering around the big table again. Apparently having learned nothing from the previous evening, virtually everyone was drinking, which either spoke to their utter stupidity or the Australian cultural dedication to casual alcoholism. On the upside, everyone looked remarkably well recovered after Cocktail Night, but there are clearly a few hangovers still being suffered. Not that this seemed to be stopping anyone from drinking. Hair of the dog that bit you, I guess.

Mum, in a rare display of common sense and decency, had planned a light meal for everyone. Dad was set up at the barbecue, grilling marinated chicken breast fillets while Mum was doling out freshly made garden salads. As we all ate, I took the opportunity to look around at the assembled crowd.

Grandma Flo and Drew were making a big show of being lovey-dovey in front of everyone, but I noticed that in the occasional unguarded moment, the two appeared to be slightly uncomfortable with each other. Drew especially, was making a point of avoiding looking in Bree's direction, with Bree doing the same to Drew.

I noticed Liam was still here. He was once again seated at the other end of the table to me, apparently keeping a respectful distance. Unlike last night, he looked very different. Gone are the shy smiles and quick glances in my direction. Now he just looks sad. Perhaps my words this afternoon had been a bit harsh. But considering our history, he would have a hell of a cheek to complain about me being unhappy with him. If anything, this seems to reinforce Bree's idea of us needing closure. Although, I doubt we'll get a chance to speak privately tonight.

As for the rest of the family, Uncle Perry is bemoaning how few people have tried his fruit mince pies; Uncle Jack is dressed up as a reindeer with glow-in-the-dark antlers; Aunty Joss looks like she wants the ground to swallow her up, and my cousin Josh is shirtless yet again, but looking visibly ill. I attribute this to him eating one of his father's pies, possibly just to keep the old man happy. Bet he regrets that now.

Once everyone is finished eating and the dishes are cleared away, Mum announces with her usual pomp and circumstance that Games Night is about to begin. Everyone but me cheers.

"But first, we have to decide what game we shall be playing this year!" Mum says.

As per usual, the annual game is decided with a dramatic random draw ceremony. Mum puts the names of dozens of party games into a large red velvet bag, shakes it up, then draws one out at random. If things fizzle out, Mum reserves the right to draw another game from the bag, but this usually only happens when everyone is severely hungover from Cocktail Night and nobody can concentrate on what's happening.

Previous years have seen the Nolan family play everything from Pictionary to Hide and Seek. Monopoly to Celebrity Heads. Each game is played with the kind of ruthlessness and ferocity that could turn an innocent game of tiddlywinks into a full-blown bloodsport. My family never did anything by halves.

Mum returned to the patio holding the velvet bag, doing her best Adriana Xenides impression, waving her hands dramatically around the bag as if she were modelling it on a cheesy eighties gameshow. The crowd cheered again.

"So, what kind of game are we likely to be playing?" Bree asks as Mum basks in the adulation of her captive audience.

"Who knows. One year it was Blind Man's Buff and three people ended up in the emergency room with broken bones. Last year, Mum lost at Monopoly and she put Uncle Jack in a headlock until he confessed to cheating. Just pray for something benign."

Bree looked at me with a mixture of horror and confusion, like perhaps I was kidding. "I wonder what will happen if she draws out Trivial Pursuit?" she asks absently.

I shuddered at the thought of Games Night 2011, and casually wonder if Uncle Perry was still passing those little plastic wedges. I send up a silent prayer that whatever Mum drew out, that it was something with a low potential for drama or fights.

We returned our attention to Mum, who had her arm in the bag and was making a big show of trying to grab one of the folded up pieces of paper within. She pulled one out, discarded the bag and slowly started to unfold the small square of notepaper.

"...and this year, our annual Games Night game shall be... drumroll please... Truth or Dare!"

Shit.

We're dead.

Chapter Nine – Truth or Consequences

I CAN'T EVEN begin to imagine how many ways a game of Truth or Dare could possibly go wrong when played by the Nolan family. Seriously, was my mother out of her fucking mind when she put this option in the velvet bag? How could she seriously think this was going to end well?

Despite the very obvious cloud of doom that now hung over the Nolan house, my family seemed to be in no way disturbed by this turn of events. In fact, they all appeared to be happy and excited to play this game. This was the first time Truth or Dare had been pulled out of the bag, so I guess many of them figured a new game would result in a new outcome. I'll give my family their due; they are relentlessly positive even in the face of overwhelming odds to the contrary.

Mum, as master of ceremonies, decided to get the game rolling by selecting the first player.

"Okay, Joss! Truth or Dare?"

Mum's sister looks at her aghast, probably wondering why she was being singled out to go first. But Aunty Joss wasn't one to shy away from a challenge.

"I choose... Dare!"

"I dare you to..." Mum takes a moment to stroke her imaginary beard to signify she was thinking up something monstrous, "...do the Macarena for thirty seconds!"

Everyone but Joss laughs. Joss hated the Macarena ever since the wretched song was released a few decades ago, and Mum knew this. Opening shots have been fired. Joss stood up and, when Mum started playing the song on her phone speaker, awkwardly began doing the dance steps for thirty seconds, then took a bow as the crowd cheered.

"Well done, Joss. Now it's your turn to pick the next player."

Joss looks around the room, her eyes narrowed as she looks for someone that will serve as a brutal counterattack. She stops when she comes to me and smiles ever so slightly.

Oh, dear...

"Charlie! Truth or Dare?" she says, sounding almost innocent.

I know that Aunty Joss would never make me do anything horrible just to get back at Mum, but I know she has something up her sleeve. So I decided to give her the benefit of the doubt.

"Dare."

"I dare you to kiss your girlfriend, Bree, for thirty seconds!"

Wow. Aunty Joss was a savage. Mum looked like she'd swallowed a particularly bitter lemon.

"Ew! Girls germs!" I cried out, but Bree simply grabbed my head with both hands and damn near sucked my face off, as the family cat called and cheered. When she released me from her vice-like grip, I dragged in a massive lungful of air.

"Damn, woman! Is your family name Dyson?" I said, wiping the lipstick off my mouth. Bree laughed and playfully slapped my shoulder.

As the game continued, I was more than a little surprised at how low-key and friendly things were playing out. However, it didn't take long for the game to start taking a turn toward menacing. Soon the questions and dares, which had started out silly, funny or cheeky, were quickly becoming a lot less friendly.

It also hadn't escaped my attention that my friend's competitive nature was out on full display. Whether it was the adrenaline junkie within Bree coming out to play, or the fact she had just knocked back her fourth scotch and cola in less than an hour, a distinctly aggressive tone had crept into my friend's voice that could only lead to trouble.

"Bree, sweetheart, your turn again!" Mum said.

"Okay..." Bree mumbled speculatively as she made a big show of surveying the faces gathered around the table. Despite her attempts to make it look like she was trying to make up her mind who would play next, I could tell she had already made her decision and was simply building up tension.

"Liam! Truth or Dare?" she eventually said.

Liam up until this point had not really been participating in the game. He had simply been watching in the background, looking distracted. But when Bree called his name, he snapped back to attention with a look of genuine shock that he would be called upon to play.

"Me?"

"Yes, you," Bree said.

"Um, okay. Truth."

Bree smirked smugly, "Why did you cheat on Charlie all those years ago?"

The whole table fell silent.

"Bree!" I admonished, wondering what the hell she was doing.

"Cheat?" Liam said, scowling at Bree, "I never cheated on anyone! What the fuck?"

"Oh come on! There's no sense in denying it..." Bree slurred indignantly.

"Bree, this isn't the time for this!" I said to her, desperately trying to avoid an ugly public scene.

"Bullshit. Let him explain himself in front of everyone."

"Charlie, why would you think I cheated on you?" Liam asked, looking absolutely shellshocked.

Internally, I was trying to maintain my calm. This was not the time for such a discussion. But his denials were filling me with that same white-hot rage I had first felt the previous evening. How could he seriously deny his infidelity?

"Are you kidding?" I exploded, unable to maintain my temper, "All those late nights at the office? All those missed dates? How about the business trips that your boss knew nothing about? How could I think you were cheating? Give me a fucking break, Liam!"

"Oh my god…" Liam said as if I had punched him in the guts. He looked stricken and, without another word, he left the table and went inside the house.

I was furious now. Not just at Liam, but at Bree too. She had no right to bring this up. Certainly not in the middle of a game in front of my whole family.

She needed to be punished.

"Well, since Liam had buggered off to who knows where, I guess I'll take his turn," I said, challenging anyone to object, "Bree, Truth or Dare?"

Bree all of a sudden looked a lot less confident as a game player. Possibly because it had just hit her what she had just done, or possibly because she had never seen me look so angry. I'm sure the slightly manic smile on my face wasn't helping things either.

"Um… truth?"

"Who did you wake up in bed with this morning?" I asked, savouring every moment as Bree's smiling face slowly collapsed and drained of blood.

"Oh, you bitch!" she hissed at me under her breath.

"Answer the question, or you get the punishment!" I said with vicious glee.

"Wait a minute," Mum interjected, "Bree is a guest. She shouldn't…"

"Oh no! She wanted to experience a real Nolan Family Christmas. She doesn't get a 'get out of jail free' card now…" I declare. Mum stands and heads into the kitchen.

"What is the punishment?" Bree asks, almost afraid to ask.

I grin evilly.

Mum returns moments later baring the platter of dodgy fruit mince pies.

"Answer – or eat a pie," I said with grim finality.

The whole table gasped.

"You know, I really resent my pies being used in this manner." Uncle Perry grumbles.

I stared down at Bree. She stared back at me, her eyes filled with bitter resolve. Without breaking eye contact, she grabbed one of the revolting pastries and carefully lifted it to her lips. Light muttering could be heard coming from the witnesses that surrounded us. Gasps of horror and disbelief as Bree opened her mouth and moved the pie toward her lips. Just as she was about to take her first bite, she hesitated.

"I can't! I can't do it! That damn thing stinks to high heaven! I woke up with Drew this morning!" Bree shrieked, dropping the pie and collapsing into a heap on the table, sobbing.

The assembled crowd erupted into gasps again. My grandmother was incredulous.

"My Drew? But that's not possible! He was in bed with me all night."

"Sorry, Grandma. But I walked in on Bree and Drew in bed together early this morning. Just after sunrise."

"But Drew was cuddled up in bed with me when I woke up. I remember us leaving the patio last night and going to bed in the guest house."

Drew, who was blushing bright red and looking guilty as sin, hung his head in shame. "I woke up early in Bree's room. Once I realised I'd gone to bed in the wrong room, I quickly sneaked back to the guest house. Flo was alone in bed, fast asleep."

This didn't make any sense. Although the fact the whole family was smashed on those lethal cocktails, it wasn't in the least bit surprising. But one thing needed to be explained.

"If Drew was in bed with Bree all night. Who was in bed with Grandma Flo?" I asked, looking around the room. Everyone seemed to look equally confused. Everyone – except my cousin Josh, who was currently staring at the floor and appeared to be hoping it would swallow him whole. He slowly raised his hand.

"You slept with Grandma?!?" I shrieked.

"We were both drunk!" Josh said, as if this explained everything, "We didn't know what we were doing! I'm pretty sure nothing happened between us. I woke up with my clothes on!"

"Oh sure, nothing happened!" My mother yelled at him, then turned to her mother, "and as for you, you wrinkled old pervert! It's bad enough you chasing young boys all over town, but now you've gotta start chasing after your own grandchildren?!?"

"I swear, it's not what you think! I don't remember a thing!" Grandma wailed. The whole room erupted into accusations and explanations. A full-blown Nolan Family drama was born.

"Um... I think it's my turn again." Bree said, wiping her eyes and trying desperately to hide a smug grin.

Oh shit.

"Truth or Dare, Charlie?"

Considering the kind of twisted dares my friend could concoct in that cold, malevolent brain of hers, I decided to go with the safer option and chose 'Truth.'

"Where did you hide your mother's cake forks?" Bree said, smiling wide like an evil clown.

"I knew you stole them!" my Mum shrieked.

You know that phrase 'If looks could kill?' I can't help but think it was invented specifically for situations like this. Because if looks could kill, my friend Bree would be a pile of dust right now, blowing away on the evening breeze.

"Never mind waking up with my Grandmother's fiance. Tomorrow morning, you'll be waking up with a dead horse's head in your bed!" I muttered under my breath as Bree delighted in her victory.

Chapter Ten – The Aftermath

AS WAS TRADITION, Games Night had devolved into little more than petty bickering and dramatic accusations. The whole family was at each other's throats. Grandma Flo was outraged at Drew and Bree; Mum was outraged at her mother and Josh, and everyone seemed to be angry at Bree for triggering this whole mess in the first place. Everyone else seemed to be just taking sides and yelling incoherently. All of this was familiar territory when it came to Christmas. But the drunken, incestuous bed-hopping was a new low, even for our family.

Ho Ho Ho...

Bree and I took advantage of a brief lull in the melee to escape the patio and go upstairs. I was still angry at her for confronting Liam and revealing the whole cake forks thing, and she was clearly mad that I threw her under the bus about the whole sleeping with Drew thing. I had to admit, even I thought I was a bit of a bastard for doing that to her, but in that moment I was just so pissed off, I wanted her to suffer a little. But how could I have ever anticipated my momentary snarkiness chain reacting and leading to the revelations we had witnessed earlier that evening?

As we approached my room in silence, I noticed a light coming from under the closed door to Liam's room. Clearly, he was still here. I couldn't figure out why. What was his game? Why was he denying his infidelity after all these years? Why was he here at all? I didn't understand why the past couldn't just remain in the past.

"Charlie, I'm so sorry about what I said downstairs," Bree said as she sat down on the bed, looking genuinely contrite, "It wasn't my place to confront Liam about anything."

"I'm sorry I told Grandma about you and Drew. It was petty and shameful. Can you ever forgive me?"

"Only if you can forgive me." Bree stood and pulled me into a big hug. "I can't believe how I behaved down there. I've never acted like that in my entire life. What the hell got into me?"

"It's this house," I assured her, "I'm pretty sure it was built on a vortex to Hell. But that's the Mornington Peninsula for you. I'm a perfectly rational, normal person all year. But the second I enter this house, it's like the Nolan crazy waves infect me and I turn into a lunatic. We should hire an exorcist."

Bree laughs as she squeezes me tight. Finally, after all these years, she sees what I've been talking about when I refer to my family's bouts of group insanity at Christmas. For so long, I'm sure Bree thought I was exaggerating, but now having witnessed it first hand, and even got swept up in their tidal wave of drama, she finally gets it.

"How did a simple party game turn into the script for a Mexican telenovela?" Bree asked, both amused and dumbfounded.

"It's Christmas!" I say in that same, drawn-out drawl my mother uses to explain the demented behaviours of the yuletide season, dragging a giggle from my friend.

"Hey, let's agree to no more secrets – at least until after the holidays?" I suggested. Bree grinned and nodded.

"Well, in that case, there's something I should tell you," Bree began, "After I woke up with Drew, he and I got to talking and..."

A soft knock at the door interrupted our conversation. I opened the door to find Liam looking solemn and a little apprehensive.

"I'm sorry, I know you probably don't want to see me. But I think we need to talk. I need to tell you some important stuff. Do you mind if we speak privately?"

I looked back at Bree who just nodded at me, somehow silently conveying not only that everything was good between us, but that she thought it was a good idea if Liam and I went and finally cleared the air. I turned back to him and silently followed him to his room.

~

Liam made himself comfortable, sitting on the bed, while I sat on the office chair next to my brother's old study desk. I wasn't sure if it was the late hour or if I was just emotionally exhausted from everything downstairs, but I couldn't summon up the anger I had felt earlier. I was just blank and ready to listen to whatever Liam wanted to say.

"Firstly," Liam started, "I want to apologise for lying to you all those years ago. All those excuses for cancelling plans and fake business trips. It's no wonder you thought I was cheating on you. But I want to assure you, I never did. Not once. Maybe, if I had been in a better headspace at the time, I would have realised the kind of impression my lies were leaving on you, and I would have explained myself better. But regardless, I'm sorry for lying to you, and even more sorry for hurting you."

I wasn't really sure how to process that. He didn't cheat on me? But he lied about where he was and what he was doing?

"Secondly, I'd like the opportunity to explain what really happened. Why I lied to you and to ask for your forgiveness."

"Okay, so what really happened?"

"Do you remember Rory?"

"Your older brother?"

"Yeah. Well, Rory had always been the black sheep of the family. He was always getting himself into trouble, even when we were kids. But after I moved out of home, I didn't really have much to do with him. Not until I got a phone call one day from my mother, asking me to come around to their place that evening. It was really strange. It was a weeknight, and there was no notice. Mum wouldn't explain what was going on, she just begged me to come along.

"So I did. When I showed up, my parents quickly explained that they had discovered my brother was a drug addict, and that this was an intervention. I was shellshocked. I hadn't been given a moment to prepare before Rory showed up, completely unaware of what was going to transpire. For the next hour, my parents berated him, accused him and demanded he go into a rehab clinic that they would pay for. My brother, who was clearly high and in no mood for this conversation, refused."

"What happened?" I asked.

"My parents told him if he didn't go into rehab immediately, they would be done with him. I suggested that my parents cool down before they say anything they would end up regretting, but they were stubborn and wouldn't back down. Rory told them to go to hell and stormed off. My parents kept their word and cut him off completely.

"Rory went off the grid. By this stage, he was homeless. He slept on friend's couches when he could, or on the streets when he couldn't. I wanted to help my brother, but he was difficult to find. I tried to file a Missing Persons report, but the police didn't take the case of a missing homeless drug addict too seriously. I begged my parents to help find him, but they wouldn't even acknowledge his existence. They told me I should stop wasting my time on 'some useless junkie.' They even went as far as to suggest that if I didn't drop it, they would cut me off too. I didn't care. I didn't need their money or their lousy parenting.

"I spent the next few weeks looking for Rory. Every spare moment I had was devoted to following leads and chasing up sightings. I even took time off work to spend more time searching for him. All the while, my obsession with finding my brother was coming at the expense of my relationship with you. When you finally told me things weren't working out and you broke up with me, I was shocked, but I couldn't bring myself to tell you why I had been so disconnected."

"Why? I don't understand why you didn't just tell me what was happening?" I couldn't get my head around this point. Why was it such a big secret?

"How could I tell you? My own parents turned their back on me for trying to help my brother. We'd barely been together for six months and I didn't want to lose you too. So I kept the whole thing quiet, hoping I would find Rory quickly and get him the help he needed."

"You thought I would turn my back on you? That would never have happened. Your parents were bastards. Always were. I never said it before, but I hated your parents when I first met them. They used their wealth and influence to do whatever they wanted. I was shocked that you were so different from them."

"Yeah, I never got into the whole high society, rich man / poor man thing. I guess in many ways, my brother wasn't the only black sheep in the family."

"So did you find Rory?"

Liam's face was suddenly ashen, and I instantly regretted asking that question.

"About a month or so after we broke up, I tracked him down to an abandoned warehouse over in the Docklands. A lot of homeless people at the time used it as a place to sleep. I went down there one night searching for him. It was dark, and it stank, but I went through the whole place. Eventually, I found him. He was dead with a needle in his arm."

"I'm so sorry, Liam." I stood and quickly embraced him in a hug. "I can't imagine how that must have been for you."

"It was worse afterwards," he said, his eyes wet and his voice wavering, "When I told my parents, they reacted like I had told them my dentist appointment had been cancelled. They showed no emotion what so ever. I tell them their eldest son is dead, and they couldn't have cared less. I never spoke to them again after that. I couldn't stomach being part of a family that was so cold and cruel, that they wouldn't even show up to their own child's funeral."

"As I said, they were bastards. That just confirms it."

All these years, I had thought Liam was a cheating scumbag, when all along he had been selflessly and singlehandedly trying to save his brother. I couldn't wrap my head around it. For so long, I had hated him. If only the two of us had talked it out.

"Hang on. How come you're only telling me this now? It's been eight years. Why didn't you contact me sooner?"

"Actually, I tried," he said sheepishly, "It took me a long time to get over Rory's death and all the crap that went down with my family. By the time I had sorted myself out and realised what a horrible mistake I'd made by letting you walk away – it had been nearly three years. I was just working up the courage to give you a call, when..."

"When what?"

"Well, I was out to dinner one night at some fancy place in the city. Just as I was finishing my meal, you walked in with a man. I watched from the other side of the restaurant for a few minutes, but it was clear you two were on a date. I realised I'd waited too long. You had moved on with your life. So I decided to just let it be."

"I don't even remember that night. Chances are it was one of my many first dates that started out lovely but inevitably ended in disaster."

"I knew I should have called you!" he said, chastising himself, "I knew I should have just picked up the phone. God, why was I such a wimp back then?"

"We both had really crap communication skills back then. We both turned our backs on our relationship when we should have just spoken to each other about our problems. We could have saved ourselves so much pain."

"We were kids," Liam said sadly, "But I'd like to think I've matured over the years. Learned from my mistakes."

"God, we wasted so much time. So many years that we could have been together. I feel like such an idiot."

Liam looked deep into my eyes. His hands rose to my face and he gently held my head, his thumbs wiping away the tears I hadn't realised I had shed. For the first time in eight years, I felt that spark; that connection between us that had been so wonderful. He slowly pressed his lips to mine. It was soft and sweet. Like taking a sip of fine wine. The taste was familiar and just as intoxicating.

"Wow," I said, unable to say anything more articulate.

"Yeah." Liam agreed. "Do you think two people can have a second chance? To have a do-over and try to get it right?"

"It's been eight years. We're very different people now. Our lives have gone in different directions. I don't think we should rush into anything."

"Well, let's just take things one step at a time then."

Liam leaned in and kissed me again, this time with a little more heat. I kissed him back, opening my mouth slightly when his tongue gently rubbed against my lips, begging admittance. It was the most passionate and sensual kiss of my life.

Chapter Eleven – Christmas Day

CHRISTMAS MORNING IN the Nolan house was far from overflowing with the holiday spirit. The events of the previous evening along with the memories of drunken incestuous bed-hopping, crippling hangovers, secrets exposed and long-held suspicions confirmed having swept away any possibility of Christmas cheer – replacing it with an unmistakable undertone of seething resentment, passive-aggressive recriminations and outright hostility.

Without really trying, we had somehow managed to, by our own low standards, break all previous records and pull off the worst Nolan Family Christmas to date.

"Drew packed his bags and left late last night," Mum informed us as Liam and I entered the kitchen for breakfast. She went on to explain that Grandma had gone straight to bed without so much as another word to anyone. Despite her best efforts to keep up a party atmosphere, Mum was unable to salvage Games Night, and the family quickly either went home or retired to bed.

So far, besides Mum and Dad, it seemed only Liam and I had emerged, so we helped ourselves to coffee. But as I raised the precious liquid to my lips, my mother interrupted.

"Uh uh uh! No coffee until you had them over!"

I rolled my eyes, knowing exactly what she was talking about. I could kill Bree for spilling my secret. I got up from my chair, got down under the kitchen table and unstrapped the box of cake forks from where I had secured them with heavy-duty duct tape. I placed them on the table and muttered an apology.

"What was that?" my mother crowed, "I didn't quite catch that."

"I said, 'I'm sorry'" I repeated, feeling more like a petulant teenager than I had in years. Liam watched on with an amused smirk.

"Such a bad boy! Don't worry, Mrs Nolan, I'll get him back on the straight and narrow!" Liam said, sipping his coffee with a cocky grin. I was tempted to take some of the duct tape and put it across his mouth – but that might make kissing him a bit more difficult.

Liam and I had ended up spending most of the night catching up on everything we had missed in each other's lives during our eight years apart. We talked about our jobs, our friends and our families. We talked about the good times and the painful times. And we had held each other throughout it all. It had been amazing. That connection that had drawn me to him all those years ago was still there, strong as ever. But despite that, we both still believed that taking things slowly was a wise choice. *Fools rush in* and all that.

Waking up that morning, cuddled in his arms, had been glorious. It wasn't sexual. It was comfortable. It was the two of us allowing our intimacy to reconnect. It was slow and sensual, like falling in a dream. Neither of us feeling pressured to say or do anything. Just experiencing the moment. Mutually agreeing to allow things to unfold naturally. In that moment, I couldn't remember a time that I had ever felt so content.

"So…" Mum said, "You and Liam?" she smirked knowingly.

"Yes, me and Liam. We're taking things one step at a time." I said, hating the fact that Mum's interference in my personal affairs had actually had a positive benefit.

"Do you have something you'd like to say to me?"

"Yes. Thanks for once again sticking your nose in where it doesn't belong. For once it wasn't a complete disaster."

"Charlie!" Mum said with manufactured outrage, "Don't be so horrible, it's Christmas!"

"I mean it, Mum. If you ever involve yourself in my personal life again, I guarantee you'll never have a problem locating your cake forks..."

"Charlie!" Dad barked not looking up from his newspaper, "Don't threaten to do unnatural things to your mother with cake forks."

"Jeez, Dad. You really know how to suck all the fun out of Christmas."

~

Breakfast with the family was... uncomfortable. Unlike in previous years, nobody seemed keen on speaking. Grandma Flo was yet to emerge from the guest house. Uncle Perry and Josh were clearly not speaking to one another. Josh's eyes rarely left his plate, so unwilling he was to make eye contact with anyone. Uncle Jack emerged from the guest house dressed in an elaborate snowman costume, featuring diamante ice crystals, a light-up carrot nose and what appeared to be real coal buttons. Aunt Joss followed behind him, shaking her head, seemingly having failed in persuading her husband to give up on the costumes. My parents were busy cooking and serving up a light breakfast for everyone, which left the majority of the conversation to Liam, Bree and myself.

And nobody wanted to talk to Bree.

It seemed the Nolan family had universally decided to blame my friend for everything that had transpired the night before, while perversely ignoring their own hand in events. Personally, I thought they were being more than just a little bit unfair. But I could also see how Bree, being an outsider, was the perfect scapegoat. That being said, Bree took it all in her stride, letting their silent seething resentment fall over her like water off a duck's back.

Despite our best attempts, we were unable to get a conversation going with anyone. The silence around the breakfast table was deafening, and I could almost feel the bubbling tension that threatened to break through the surface at any given moment. However, the meal ultimately passed without incident.

After breakfast, Bree elected to help Mum and Joss put the salads together for lunch, while Liam and I decided to take a quick walk down to the nearby beach to get some fresh air. It was still early enough in the morning that the temperature was warm without being stifling, and the cool ocean breeze was bracing.

Liam and I stripped down to our swim shorts and we took a quick dip in the cool water. The refreshing chill of the ocean and the tang of the salt in the air when I emerged from the water made my skin tingle. I looked over and watched as Liam walked out of the crashing waves. The water droplets that clung to his chest slowly ran down his torso, almost in slow motion, as they flowed down his muscular stomach. My breath hitched, overcome by the sheer beauty of the man. Liam met my gaze, catching me mid-ogle and winked cheekily at me as he casually brushed his wet hair back from his face.

He took a moment to ogle me back, but his smile faltered as he looked at my lower belly. He came over, his eyes filled with concern.

"What's this?" he asked, gently tracing the scar with his fingertips. "What happened to you?"

"I had my appendix out a few years ago. I was in the hospital for a few days, but I was lucky not to suffer too much. Appendectomies are apparently a lot more dangerous in adults."

"I can't believe how much I've missed. I wish I had known…"

"Well, what about you? Missing any internal organs?" I said, trying to lighten the mood. Liam instantly smiled.

"Not that I know of. Although, there was that one weekend in Surfer's Paradise…"

"What?"

"Well, I went out drinking with some mates, got completely blitzed out of my mind. I woke up the next morning in a motel room, lying in a bathtub filled with ice…" Liam tried to remain straight-faced, but couldn't stifle his giggle.

"Smart arse!" I laughed and playfully smacked his shoulder. "C'mon. We better get back to the house. It'll be lunch soon. I have feeling this is going to be one for the record books."

We gathered our things and made our way back up the beach. As we walked, Liam asks if I'm okay after everything that happened the previous night. I assure him that I am and that these things happen every year. Admittedly, not nearly as spectacularly as this year. But balance would eventually be restored.

Although, after the events of the last few days, it would take a miracle to rescue this Christmas from the dumpster fire it was currently luxuriating in.

Chapter Twelve – Cracks and Crackers

I HAD TO hand it to my mother, she had certainly outdone herself this year. When we were all finally allowed to go downstairs to the rumpus room, the whole space had been completely transformed. Gone was Dad's dark and dingy 'man cave.' In its place, a light, bright room decorated with elegant white twinkle lights, a fancy silver Christmas tree surrounded by dozens of wrapped presents; and a long, carefully set up dining table.

The table was set with Mum's best china, cutlery and glassware. All the fancy stuff that was usually carefully packed away the rest of the year. Cloth napkins with silver rings, a beautifully polished candelabra and an intricate centrepiece made of holly and pinecones. There were even individual gold and silver Christmas crackers serving as place cards, designating where each person was to sit. Mum always went posh at Christmas, but this year she had gone the extra mile. I almost felt like I should be dressed in a tuxedo just to eat lunch.

Dad's bar fridge had been filled with an assortment of drinks including beer, wine, champagne and soft drinks. The whole thing was topped off with a CD of classic Christmas carols played softly in the background – enough for atmosphere but without being obtrusive.

But best of all, at the far end of the room, was Mum's famous running buffet. A series of tables, lined up in a long row, covered with a feast of festive treats. Rather than trying to individually cater to each person, the buffet allowed everyone to serve themselves in their own time, allowing Mum and Dad to enjoy the meal they had worked so hard to put together.

Since Australians get to celebrate Christmas in the middle of Summer, most families don't bother with serving a hot meal on the big day. But a lot of the traditional foods, such as turkey, roast beef and ham are served as cold cuts alongside the usual trimmings like roast potatoes and gravy. But the meal is also rounded off with a variety of salads and fresh seafood like prawns, Balmain bugs and cracked crabs. Mum clearly thought she was feeding an army rather than just her family.

Speaking of army, when Liam and I returned from the beach, I caught Mum having a moment in the kitchen. I knew immediately why she was upset. It happened every year. With my older brother, Craig, on deployment, the only chance of seeing him over the holidays would be a brief phone or video call at some point. Because of operational security, we weren't allowed to know where my brother was or even when (or if) he would be calling us. The wait was always hardest on Mum, who so desperately wanted to know her eldest child was safe. Without a word, I scooped Mum up into my arms and held her. After a few seconds, she kissed my cheek, told me I was a 'good boy,' and went about stirring something on the stove, as if nothing had happened.

Lunch was reasonably peaceful, all things considered. Everyone seemed to be getting along relatively well. Although I knew from experience this was merely a ceasefire. Once lunch was over, hostilities would resume. As our plates slowly emptied, the resentments that had been building up over the last day or so were starting to show. Mum was sneering at Grandma. Grandma continued to shoot daggers at Bree. Uncle Perry kept a close eye on his son, while my cousin Josh avoided making eye contact with anyone. Bree kept her eyes on her plate, apparently determined not to make a bad situation worse.

In stark contrast to the rest of my family, Liam and I kept looking at each other and smiling goofily like a pair of lovestruck teenagers. This had not gone unnoticed by my mother, who briefly stopped sneering at her mother to smile smugly at me. I knew it wouldn't be long before the tranquillity of the meal was shattered, and it would be my Grandmother who was destined to fire the first shot.

"Pass the salt," she said, scowling at Bree.

"Say please, Mother!" my mother gently admonished.

"Fine. Would the home-wrecking slut *please* pass the salt?"

"Grandma!" I said.

"What?" she said with pseudo-innocence.

"You know what?" Bree said, finally snapping, dropping her cutlery on her plate with a clatter, "I wasn't going to say anything. I was going to keep my mouth shut and preserve your dignity. But if you wanna start calling me names, maybe I don't owe you a damned thing."

My grandmother continued to scowl, not willing to give an inch.

"What are you talking about?" Mum asked, looking puzzled.

"When I woke up with Drew, he and I got to talking. Seems, he's not your fiance after all. He's a hired escort."

The room was filled with the sound of shocked gasps. Grandma turned bright red from embarrassment. My mother turned red from fury.

"So do let me know how much you paid for your man-whore, Flo," Bree said, spitting as much acid into her words as she possibly could, "I'll give you a refund. Then you can afford to hire a new 'fiance.' That is, if you aren't too busy sleeping with your own grandchildren!"

The room was so silent, you could hear a pin drop. Grandma looked like she was going to explode, and my mother looked like she was going to faint.

"Mother!" Mum shrieked, "Escorts? Why? Why would you do such a thing?"

"To drive you nuts!" Grandma yelled, her face a study of unrepentant fury, "Every year, we have to go through this ridiculous routine of you 'organising' the hell out of Christmas. Everything has to be *so* perfect. Everything has to be *so* fancy. I'm sick of it!"

"What's wrong with having a nice Christmas?" Mum said, sounding almost heartbroken.

"Look around, Kathleen! Your husband was a miner. I spent forty years working on a factory assembly line. We're not fancy people. Yet, every single year, you go out of your way to make everything as posh and over-the-top as you can – and simultaneously suck all the fun out of everything with your rules and schedules."

Mum sat down in her chair, looking deflated.

"I just wanted everyone to have a good time. I just wanted us to have the perfect Christmas," she said, her voice barely a whisper.

"There's no such thing as a 'perfect' Christmas! I don't know why we can't just do what we always do with family get-togethers. Just relax and enjoy ourselves. No schedules. No organised 'fun.' Just spend time together as a nice, normal family..."

"Wait a minute," Mum said, suddenly appearing a lot less defeated all of a sudden, "You sneaky old bitch! You're just saying all this to distract everyone from the fact that you've been hiring hookers!"

Grandma turned beet red.

Busted!

I swear to God, I tried not to laugh, but between watching Bree lose her temper and go on the attack, and my Mum finally scoring a few points against her mother, I couldn't hold back anymore. When I started to giggle, it wasn't long before others in the room started snickering. Eventually, the whole room burst into uproarious laughter, much to my Grandmother's chagrin. Once the laughter died down, Flo stood up and scowled at everyone.

"How can you all be so cruel? I can't believe how you're all behaving. It's Christmas and you're all being so beastly to me. Not one of you loves me!" she shrieked.

"I still love you, Grandma." a voice said from the staircase at the far end of the room. Everyone turned to see a man in full army uniform standing at the foot of the stairs.

My brother.

"Um, surprise! Merry Christmas, everyone!"

Chapter Thirteen – A Christmas Miracle

I HAVE NEVER before seen the mood of a room shift so seismically, so quickly. Only moments earlier, my whole family were morose, angry and even verbally sparring with each other. Now suddenly, all petty grievances were forgotten; all feuds were set aside. The entire room erupted in an explosion of love and excitement to see my brother home – safe and sounds.

Craig opened his arms and, losing any sense of decorum or grace, Mum flew across the room and practically crash-tackled him. He embraced her in a tight hug as she sobbed uncontrollably with pure, unrestrained joy. Before long, the whole family was mobbing Craig in a sort of awkward group hug.

Eventually, the crowd dispersed enough to allow Craig to breathe a little, and everyone greeted him individually. Dad had wet eyes as he pulled his son into his arms, slapping his back in that blokey way all straight men do when they hug. Craig then embraced Grandma and she grabbed his head with both hands, peppering his face with kisses.

When I approached Craig, I couldn't hold back the tears as I grabbed hold of him tight. All those nights I had laid awake wondering where he was, if he was safe and if he would ever come home to us. All that worry for my big brother came bubbling to the surface.

"Welcome home. Never leave again!" I managed to get out.

"I missed you too, baby bro," he whispered in my ear.

Once everyone had calmed down, Craig took a seat at the dining table while Mum fixed him a big plate of food and Dad brought him a beer.

"My tour ended early, but I wasn't sure if I was going to be allowed to return home right away or if I would be sent on to some temporary assignment. I didn't want to tell you anything until I knew one way or the other. By the time I found out for sure, I figured just showing up would be a nice Christmas surprise. That, and I'd have an excellent excuse for not buying anyone any presents!"

Everyone laughed. Mum placed an absolutely overloaded plate of food in front of her eldest son and his eye's bulged.

"Jeez, Mum. I haven't had a meal this big in a long time. This could take me a while to get through."

"That's alright, darling. I think we have a lot of catching up to do."

While Craig was able to tell us a little about his most recent tour, he wasn't allowed to talk about where he was, for how long or what he did there. Everyone understood, but that didn't stop us trying to guess. Craig was a tough cookie, though. Even if someone did guess correctly, he'd never give it away.

"So, what's all this about Grandma and man-whores?" Craig asked.

The room fell silent. Grandma baulked but quickly recovered herself.

"It's not important, dear," she said using her sweet little old lady voice, "All that matters is that you're back home with us, safe and well."

"So, 'no comment' then, eh Grandma?" Craig smirked.

"Shut up and eat your lunch dear," Grandma said with a stern voice.

"Yes ma'am," Craig said smiling as he tucked in.

~

After lunch, Liam and I went upstairs and packed up all of his stuff so my brother could have his room back. We transferred everything into my old room, then transferred Bree's stuff into my sister's vacant bedroom. That way everyone would have their own space and, more importantly, Liam and I could have some privacy. When we were done, we went back downstairs to get some fresh air in the garden.

"So, is every Nolan Family Christmas this dramatic?" Liam asked.

"This one had been a little more colourful than usual, but yes, more or less."

"Wonderful! I can't wait for the next one!"

I slapped him on the arm. "Are you insane? You can't say things like that! You'll put it out there and you'll jinx it. I don't think I could go through another Christmas like this one!"

Liam just chuckled and pulled me into a tight embrace, kissing me deeply until my toes curled.

"Merry Christmas, Charlie."

"Merry Christmas, Liam."

That evening, Mum shocked the whole family by saying that they were going to break with tradition that night. Normally, Christmas Night was Carol Night, where we would all be expected to sit around singing classic Christmas carols, drinking brandy and trying not to comment on each other's horrible singing. So you can imagine everyone's surprise when Mum suggested we have a family slumber party downstairs in the rumpus room.

Considering how exhausted everyone was, and how nobody could stomach an entire evening of musical masochism, the idea of pulling everyone's sleeping bags and blankets down to the now cleared rumpus room and watching some Christmas movies was a welcome change to the schedule.

Everyone made themselves comfortable and gathered around the big TV screen. Liam and I found a nice spot in the corner of the room; spaced well enough away so we got a good view of the TV while also being in the range of the gloriously cool air conditioner. Mum picked a DVD at random and selected *Home Alone 2: Lost in New York*. The combination of Christmas cheer and unrelenting psychopathic violence seemed oddly appropriate this year.

Once everyone was settled and snuggled down, the lights dimmed and the movie began. It didn't take us long to realise that everyone was already asleep before the opening credits had even finished. Liam and I snuggled down, watched the movie, then quietly went upstairs, leaving my peacefully slumbering family to it.

~

Up until this point, I hadn't wanted to do anything too passionate with Liam because we had been sleeping in my brother's old room. Maybe it was just me, but there was something just a little bit creepy about using my sibling's childhood bedroom for getting it on with my long lost boyfriend. But with Craig's homecoming and Liam and I being able to reclaim my old room, that feeling of discomfort had finally melted away.

I had initially suggested Liam and I share a shower, an activity we had both long ago enjoyed. But I quickly changed my mind when I remembered how small the ensuite bathroom in my old room was. Let's just say there wouldn't be anything erotic about two grown men trying to cram themselves into a shower cubical the size of a coffin. We decided taking turns showering was the more practical option.

Once showered, Liam and I cuddled up in the double bed. As a teenager, I remember how grown up and spacious the bed had been. Now, as an adult, trying to accommodate my equally adult boyfriend, it seemed a lot smaller. But having Liam crammed up against me, our naked forms rubbing against each other, the size of the mattress was the last thing on my mind.

Since neither of us had considered the need to bringing supplies with us, we would just have to improvise when it came to our lovemaking. This suited me since I wasn't quite ready for full penetrative sex after all these years. I was more than happy for us to explore our bodies and rediscover all those little places that made each other shake with desire.

I climbed on top of Liam and straddled his narrow hips. Liam slowly ran his hands down my back, starting at my neck and smoothing his way down until he cupped my buttocks. He applied the gentlest pressure to my hole with his finger and I had to stifle a gasp. He smiled wolfishly, knowing full well the reaction I would have. He moved his fingers down to behind my balls and tapped the patch of skin there, triggering another moan from me. Liam clearly remembered the spots guaranteed to get me going. Two could play at that game.

I smoothed my hands over the vast plains of his lightly furred chest. I found his nipples and gently flicked them, one by one, each time eliciting an almost surprised gasp from my lover. I did it again, only this time I gave both nipples a gentle squeeze and tug. Without conscious thought, Liam's hips bucked up and I could feel his thick cock sliding along my crack. I reached behind me and cupped his balls as he rutted against me.

Liam flipped me onto my side and lay his long body against me – his chest to my back. He lifted my leg slightly and positioned his cock between my thighs, then gently placed my leg back down. He reached around and grabbed my cock, squeezing it in that tantalising way I remembered from so many years ago. He began pumping me in time to his thrusts, kissing the back of my neck as I desperately tried to keep from crying out with pleasure.

"I'm not going to last," Liam growled, gasping from breath.

"Me neither. Come for me, baby," I said as I felt that tingle at the base of my spine that told me I was only seconds away from release. Liam's thrusts became erratic as he approached his orgasm. As we both reached the precipice, it didn't take long for both of us to tumble over in the abyss of delight.

Liam and I lay there for a few moments, panting until our breathing came under control, covered in the sticky evidence of our physical reconciliation.

"Wow," Liam said, unable to say much else at that point.

"Yeah," I agreed.

Now that was a Christmas gift I would remember for a very long time.

Chapter Fourteen – Boxing Day

BECAUSE OF ALL the excitement of Craig's homecoming, everyone had apparently forgotten all about the Christmas presents from yesterday. So first thing on Boxing Day morning, the Nolan family exchanged gifts.

Mum, as per usual, had done all her Christmas gift shopping at the Chemist Superstore down the road, so everyone got either talcum powder, cheap knock-off brand perfume or 'I can't believe it's not silk' handkerchiefs.

Mum wasn't exactly the most inspired gift giver, but she did take pride in being able to do all her gift shopping in one place for under fifty bucks. Bree gave my mother a gorgeous bottle of Cabernet. My mum gave Bree a bottle of 'Smells Just Like Britney Spears: Curious.'

The rest of my family, apparently inspired by my mother's complete lack of enthusiasm when it came to Christmas shopping, gave each other utter garbage as well. I got so much talcum powder, my balls will be dry until the end of time.

Uncle Jack distributed his gifts around the room while dressed as a penguin. The outfit, an assemblage of crafting felt, pipe cleaners and glue-on glitter, was of significantly lower quality than his previous holiday regalia. This lead me to believe his annual costume budget must have been blown on the snowman suit, leaving him to improvise this monstrosity. Aunt Joss followed in his wake, shaking her head.

"Uncle Jack," I asked carefully, "What does a penguin have to do with Christmas?"

He looked at me like I had been dropped on my head as a child, shook his head, then simply said, "Isn't it obvious?"

"Not really..."

"There were penguins on Noah's Ark!" he said in a tone that suggested this statement somehow explained his wardrobe choice. I looked to Aunt Joss, hoping she could elaborate.

"Don't look at me!" she said, rolling her eyes, "I tried to explain it to him three times, he wouldn't be told!"

I decided asking any further questions would be a waste of everyone's time, so I just nodded as if I understood then backed away slowly. Jack resumed his gift-giving, and I briefly considered placing a call to the nearest mental health professional.

Boxing Day was like spending the holiday with a different family. Craig's unexpected return home had completely turned everything around, and moods had never been lighter. Breakfast as a group was lively but contained. Everyone was happy and enjoying each other's company. No seething resentments. No arguments. No biting or knife fights. It was almost like we were a normal family, having a normal Christmas.

I decided to sit back and enjoy it while I could because it was unlikely to last. This time next year, the Nolan Family would be back to their usual, psychopathic, dramatic selves. But for now, we were happy and normal.

Just feels wrong, somehow...

~

That afternoon, Bree and I packed up our belongings and prepared to return to Melbourne. As tempting as it was to stay a few days longer and visit with my big brother, I could tell Craig was wiped out and wanted nothing more than to crash out and relax for a few days after what was likely a hellish trip home. Once the car was packed up, I left

Bree to have some tea with my parents while I went to talk with a certain handsome man in the garden.

"All ready to go?" Liam asked, standing under the large gum tree.

"Just about. I wanted to check in with you before we headed off. You're heading home today, too?"

Liam nodded. We had exchanged phone numbers and address details earlier in the day, and even set up a coffee date in the city for a few days time. But I suspected we would be in contact with each other long before then. The date was simply the first step in our 'taking it slow' plan, so we could get back into a rhythm in our normal environment.

"I can't believe after all this time, we're back together. That we got this second chance. I'm so lucky."

"I'm lucky too," Liam said, taking me in his arms, "and I'm going to do everything I can to show you how much I've missed you."

He leaned in slowly, brushing his lips against mine, clutching me tightly to his chest. A loud whooping noise came from the direction of the kitchen. We broke the kiss to see Bree and my parents smiling at us through the kitchen window.

"Crazy people," I muttered under my breath.

"Yeah, but I kind of like a bit of crazy in my life."

Mum and Dad saw us all out to our cars. Liam kissed me one last time before getting into his car and driving away. In that moment, my heart ached at his absence, but I quickly shook off the feeling. He had literally just left. I'm going to be a basket case if I don't get a grip quickly.

Dad gave me and Bree a huge hug, slapping each of us on the back in the blokey style that I was never prepared for. Bree giggled at his antics. Mum hugged me next, kissed me on the cheek and refused to let go.

"Drive safe and call me as soon as you get home."

"I promise, Mum."

"And I want to know everything about your date with Liam."

"Yes, Mum."

"I love you, darling."

"I love you too, Mum. Take care."

Bree and I got into the car and just as I started pulling out of the parking space in front of the house, there was a sharp banging on the passenger side. Bree wound down the window to reveal my mother.

"You better not of taken my cake forks again!" she bellowed with a withering scowl of warning.

"Mother, I would never do such a thing!" I said, trying for innocence. Mum looked suitably unimpressed.

"I mean it!"

"Bye, Mum!" and with that, I pulled out and sped away from Crazyland for another year.

"Did you take her cake forks?" Bree asked as we made our way to the freeway.

"Certainly not!" I said with indigence, "Her salad spoons, however..."

We both laughed as the afternoon sun streaked across the clear blue Summer sky.

Epilogue – One Year Later

"DO I HAVE TO?" I whined and Liam simply nodded, brooking no argument, "Fine!" I begrudgingly agreed. Liam had insisted that I return Mum's salad spoons as soon as we arrived at my parent's house. It was bad enough we were going to go through another four-day crazython with my family, but now he was ruining all my pettiness as well.

"You did promise to make an effort this year. Plus, both your brother *and* your sister will be coming this year, Hopefully, that will help to make Christmas run a bit smoother than last year."

I burst out laughing. Honking great guffaws. I had tears in my eyes as I struggled to breathe. I loved Liam with all of my heart, but bless his little cotton socks – he seriously believed that. I started laughing again.

"Alright, wise guy!" he said zipped up the last of our suitcases and placed it on the ground with the others. "Admittedly, that was probably a bit naive. But you could at least try to avoid provoking a confrontation."

Yeah, he was probably right. Damn it.

Ever since Liam and I moved in together three months ago, he had become the calming, sensible influence on my life. The little angel on my shoulder telling me it was probably a bad idea to send my mother round the twist for no specific reason. I nodded my agreement, and we took our bags downstairs to load into the car.

I'll put the salad spoons somewhere obvious in the kitchen so she'll find them instantly, then deny any knowledge. It'll still drive her nuts.

Mum and Dad had quite the full house when we arrived. My brother, Craig, was cuddled up on the sofa with his girlfriend, Bree.

The two of them had been inseparable since they met up last New Year's Eve. I'm still a little tickled to see the two of them so happy together.

My sister, Charmaine, had just returned home from university with her girlfriend, Robyn. Despite having loved Queensland, the two of them decided to return to Victoria where all their family and friends were. The two girls were in the kitchen with Aunt Josie, helping to make fruit mince pies. Uncle Perry had been so insulted by everyone's attitude to his culinary 'masterpieces' last year, he had refused to make the infamous pies ever again. We all let out a heavy sigh of relief.

Grandma showed up with Graham, an elderly gentleman with a short white beard and thick, coke-bottle glasses. Flo introduced him as a 'friend' however, everyone noticed how the two of them kept holding hands and stealing kisses when they thought no one was looking. I guess the events of last Christmas had put Grandma off her love of toyboys for life.

Slowly but surely, the rest of the family trickled in as they all prepared for Christmas Eve Eve and the dreaded Cocktail Night. Despite her assurances that this Christmas would be less regimented and more relaxed, my mother had refused point-blank to give up on all her traditions. So when she and Dad announced their latest creation – a lime green concoction with creamy white foam, served in oversized martini glasses – the whole family groaned collectively.

"Save me, Liam! Save me from the evil Christmas cocktail of death!" I squealed, doing my best impression of an old school damsel in distress.

"Jeez, and you call us dramatic!" my Dad said with a chuckle.

"Actually, before you render us all unconscious," Liam said, stopping my parents as they passed the glasses of vile fluid around, "Charlie and I have an announcement."

I looked at him, shocked. I didn't think we were going to do this now. "I thought we were going to wait until New Year?" I whispered to him.

"I can't wait any longer. Everyone's here. Let's do it." Liam beamed at me, excited as a kid in a toy shop.

"Okay. Everyone?" I stood up and got everyone's attention. The room fell silent. "As you know, this time last year, Liam and I reconciled after a long absence. We needed time to get to know each other again. To make sure we still worked as a couple. This last year has proven that not only do we still love each other but that our love has grown."

Everyone awwwed. It was gross. I hate that cutesy stuff.

"Anyway, we just wanted to let you know that not only do we love each other and that we are each other's soul mates – but we have also decided to get married!"

The room erupted with cheers and applause as Liam and I were engulfed in a massive Nolan tidal wave of hugs and kisses. Before I knew what was happening, Mum was telling me about this gorgeous matching pair of tuxedos she had seen in a shop in the city; Dad was shaking Liam's hand and offering him a beer; My sister was demanding to be the flower girl at the wedding and Grandma was insisting we start working on her great-grandchildren immediately. Liam looked like he was being swallowed whole by my family.

Sucked in! Should have waited until New Years. There would have been fewer people here!

"Oh, I forgot to tell you, Liam," Mum said, "The cocktails are dairy-free this year. So there are no excuses this time!" she cackled like a witch.

Liam's eyes were wide as saucers as I laughed at his expression.

"Don't worry, my love. I'll stay on the soft drink this year. Maybe this year, I'll get to clean *you* up after you vomit all over yourself while blind drunk?"

"Awww, that's so... revoltingly unromantic," Liam said with a sour face.

"That's Christmas for ya!" I said, as I placed my arms around him and kissed him deeply.

So maybe my family aren't the total nightmare I used to think they were. Despite the drama, the fights, the dangerous cocktails and the fatal pastries – there's a whole lot of love too. And without one special Family Christmas Fiasco, I wouldn't have reconnected with the man of my dreams.

Now that's what I call a Christmas miracle.

THE END

A Note From The Author

Happy Holidays to all my lovely readers and thank you for your kind support throughout what has been a troubling and difficult year for us all. I hope you enjoyed reading this fun little short story. I had a great time writing it and really enjoyed doing something a bit more comedic.

I hope you and your loved ones are safe, healthy and able to enjoy the festive season with as much normalcy as can be expected given the current circumstances.

I look forward to sharing more of my work in the new year. In the meantime, stay safe, be kind and spread the love!

Lots of Love

Alex Leslie

PS: Don't forget to follow me on social media for updates on my upcoming titles.

Twitter: http://www.twitter.com/alexleslie

Facebook: http://www.facebook.com/alexleslieauthor

Instagram: http://www/instagram.com/alexleslieauthor

Website: http://www.alexleslieauthor.com

Don't miss out!

Visit the website below and you can sign up to receive emails whenever Alex Leslie publishes a new book. There's no charge and no obligation.

https://books2read.com/r/B-A-CCJI-GZZVB

BOOKS 2 READ

Connecting independent readers to independent writers.

About the Author

Alex Leslie is an Australian-born author of Gay M/M romance works including *Chasing The Cupcake Boy, Hearts Unfrozen, Following His Bliss* and *My Big Gay Family Christmas Fiasco.*

Alex lives with his partner, two troublesome cats (who love sleeping on his laptop!) and is currently dealing with an ongoing addiction to iced coffee drinks.

Read more at www.alexleslieauthor.com.